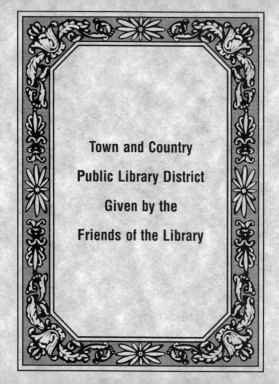

The Third Pig Detective Agency

in

The Ho Ho Ho Mystery

The THIRD PIG DETECTIVE AGENCY
THE HO HO HO MYSTERY

BOB BURKE

FRIDAY
FICTION

TOWN & COUNTRY
PUBLIC LIBRARY DISTRICT
ELBURN, IL 60119

The Friday Project
An imprint of HarperCollinsPublishers
77–85 Fulham Palace Road, Hammersmith, London W6 8JB

www.thefridayproject.co.uk
www.harpercollins.co.uk

First published by The Friday Project in 2010

1

Bob Burke asserts the moral right to be identified as the author of this work

A catalogue record for this book is available from the British Library

ISBN 978-0-00-736401-5

This novel is entirely a work of fiction. The names, characters and incidents portrayed in it are the work of the author's imagination. Any resemblance to actual persons, living or dead, events or localities is entirely coincidental.

Mixed Sources
Product group from well-managed
forests and other controlled sources
www.fsc.org Cert no. SW-COC-1806
© 1996 Forest Stewardship Council

FSC is a non-profit international organisation established to promote the
responsible management of the world's forests. Products carrying the FSC
label are independently certified to assure consumers that they come
from forests that are managed to meet the social, economic and
ecological needs of present and future generations.

Find out more about HarperCollins and the environment at
www.harpercollins.co.uk/green

Internal design and typesetting by Wordsense Ltd, Edinburgh

Printed and bound in Great Britain by Clays Ltd, St Ives plc

To Ian, Adam and Stephen

For the inspiration
(and for keeping me grounded)

Contents

1

Lady in Red

The woman claiming to be Mrs Claus glowered at me, her face turning as red as her very Christmassy jacket. 'Well,' she demanded, 'is there a problem?'

I considered the question carefully. There were a number of problems actually, but I wasn't about to list them out – at least not to a very angry woman who seemed capable of doing me serious physical harm. I'd received enough punishment during my last case and I wanted this one – if, in fact, it turned out to be a case at all – to be as pain-free as possible. Diplomacy was clearly the order of the day.

'Mrs Claus, please make yourself at home.' She squeezed herself into the offered chair, which protested loudly at the intrusion. It looked like someone had tried to stuff a red pillow into a flowerpot. When she was comfortable (or at least not too uncomfortable), I asked her to tell me the story from the beginning; if nothing else, it would give me a chance to get my thoughts together – and these thoughts were currently so far apart they couldn't even be seen with the help of the Hubble telescope.

'It's my husband, you see,' she said, fidgeting with her cuffs. 'He's disappeared.'

'And your husband would be . . . ?' I knew what she was going to say; I just wanted to hear her say it. This was obviously a very poor attempt at a practical joke and I needed to stay sharp to find out who the culprit was, although the finger of suspicion was pointing firmly at Red Riding Hood. This was just the kind of stunt she'd pull. More importantly, once I knew who it was, I could figure out a way to get back at them. No one got the better of Harry Pigg in the practical jokes department.

'He's Santa Claus, of course.' Her face got redder with indignation. 'Who did you think I was married to dressed like this?'

I had to admit she did look the part. If I had to buy an outfit for Santa's wife, it was exactly what I'd have picked: fashionable red trouser suit with white fur lining and a very trendy pair of black high-heeled boots. Well, I'd have picked something red anyway.

'OK, let me get this clear,' I said, trying hard not to snigger. 'You are married to Santa?'

'Yes,' she replied.

2

'As in the jolly fellow with the white beard who says, "Ho ho ho" a lot and flies around dropping off presents to children all over the world on Christmas Eve?'

'Is there another?' she demanded.

'Not that I'm aware of.' I was now biting the inside of my cheek so as not to laugh hysterically in her face. 'And he's missing?'

'Yes, as I've already pointed out to you.'

'You're sure he's missing and not just away on a boys' weekend with the Easter Bunny and the Tooth Fairy?' I couldn't contain myself any longer and burst into howls of laughter.

Seconds later I was pinned to the wall behind my desk with Mrs Claus's forearm rammed firmly up against my neck. I felt my eyes bulge from the pressure on my throat and I was distinctly short of breath.

'Do you think this is funny?' she demanded. 'My husband has disappeared; children all over the world are facing huge disappointment when they wake up on Christmas Day and find nothing under their trees except bare carpet and some pine needles, and you see fit to sit there making jokes at my expense?' She pulled her arm away and I dropped to the floor gasping for air. I noticed that my two new 'partners', Jack Horner and the genie, had beaten a hasty retreat into the main reception area outside. Cowards! I might have to revisit this new working arrangement if this was going to be their attitude at the slightest hint of trouble.

'Clearly I'm wasting both my time and yours, Mr Pigg,' she said, with what I must admit was a certain degree of righteous indignation. 'I shall take my business to someone who is prepared to take my problem somewhat more seriously. Good day to you.'

As she stomped to the door and made to leave, it occurred to me that she might actually be telling the truth; she was pushing it a bit for someone playing a joke. More to the point, if she was being truthful, taking her business elsewhere meant Red Riding Hood would get the case and the only way she was getting any case at my expense was over my cold and lifeless body. Then again, with my luck, that mightn't be beyond the bounds of possibility either – I'd come close a few times on my last case, why would this be any different?

It was time for eating some pie of the humbly flavoured sort.

'Mrs Claus, please accept my apologies for my behaviour.' I walked after her and extended my trotter. 'My last case has left me the worse for wear and I'm not quite myself at the moment.' If you've been keeping up with my career, you'll know this wasn't entirely untrue. 'Please make yourself comfortable and I will give you my complete and undivided attention and will personally guarantee the quality of service for which this agency is renowned.'

I was piling it on a bit, but, in my defence, I was getting desperate. I needed to keep this client. Apparently mollified, she turned and sat back down in the chair – which once more protested loudly at the strain.

I breathed a sigh of relief. 'Thank you,' I said. 'It won't happen again.'

'Make sure it doesn't,' Mrs Claus replied. 'I haven't got time for amateurs and I need to find my husband before it's too late.' Her tough veneer finally cracked and she began to cry gently.

'You mean they might kill him?'

'No,' she blubbed. 'I mean too late for Christmas.' Obviously the thought of her husband being killed hadn't crossed her mind and the tears came even more quickly when she realised what I'd said.

Nice one, Harry, I thought. *Make the client feel worse.*

I handed her a tissue from a box in my drawer and she dabbed her eyes. While she did so, I quickly checked the box to make sure I had enough tissues. I figured she could be crying for quite some time.

'Mrs Claus, perhaps you could start from the beginning so we can decide on a proper course of action. How long has he been gone?'

'Since yesterday morning,' she replied. 'He left the previous night for our northern base and was due to arrive first thing yesterday. According to the elves, he never showed. We've checked with air-traffic control and they've had no reports of any accidents. The last thing we heard was when he gave us an update an hour out of Grimmtown.

5

Since then, nothing. It's as if he just disappeared into thin air. I may never see him again.' This brought on a fresh deluge of tears. Now I was really concerned; if she didn't stop soon there was the distinct possibility my office would be flooded and I wasn't sure that my insurance would cover the cost of the damage.

'OK, OK.' I whipped out my notebook and began to scribble down what she was saying. 'How was he getting to your base? Grimmair?'

'Oh goodness, no. He always flew himself. He's quite an accomplished sleigh pilot, you know. He doesn't like travelling by commercial airlines.'

I didn't blame him. I didn't fancy it too much either. I always seemed to end up squashed between the two smelliest, loudest and most unpleasant Orcs on the flight – and they always took my peanuts.

'So, he left on his sleigh. Was this some sort of motorised craft or . . . ?'

'Goodness, Mr Pigg, do you know nothing about my husband? It was reindeer powered. All his sleighs are propelled by a team of reindeer. Of course this wasn't the elite team; they're saved for the Christmas run. These were just economy reindeer, but certainly capable enough of getting him to the North Pole without incident. But he never arrived.' More tears.

'And you've received no communication of any sort, either from him or anyone who may have taken him?'

'Nothing and I'm so worried something might have happened to him. Please, Mr Pigg, I need your help; the children need your help.'

I thought of Jack Horner waiting outside. What would he think of me if I didn't find Santa Claus – especially if I didn't do so before December 25th?

'OK, let's go through some of the more obvious questions. Does he have any enemies?'

A shake of the head.

'Have you noticed anyone suspicious hanging around the house over the past few days?'

Another shake.

'Do you know of any reason why anyone would want to kidnap him? Are you rich?'

'We have some money put aside, but we reinvest most of what we make back into the company. Every year there are new toys added to the children's lists, so we're constantly developing new products and this puts quite a drain on our finances. We're not in it for the money, you know. If whoever did this did it because they think we're wealthy, they'll be sorely disappointed.'

That left one obvious question. 'So if he wasn't kidnapped for the money, then why was he kidnapped?'

Mrs Claus shrugged and said, 'I don't know; I just want you to find him, whatever it takes.' But as she said it, I thought I detected the faintest hint of evasion in the glance she gave me. She knew more than she was saying. There was obviously something else going on here and, with my luck, it would almost certainly result in something unpleasant happening to me while I tried to work out what it was.

Super!

'Is there anything else you can tell me that might be important?' I pressed. 'Did your husband appear any different before he left? Did he seem tense, out of sorts? Any little detail, anything you might have noticed, no matter how insignificant, might be important.'

Mrs Claus thought for a second and shook her head. 'No, nothing. It was just another trip. He was as happy as always. Lots of "Ho, ho, ho's" and "Merry Christmas, everyone's". He did like to get into the spirit of things early. And now he's gone.'

Just when I thought the waterworks had finished, they started up again. She was a one-woman reservoir. She appeared to be storing enough water inside her to supply an entire town for a year. Where did she keep it all? I was hoping she'd stop soon – I was running out of tissues.

'Mrs Claus, let me assure you that the Third Pig Detective Agency is on the job. Our skilled operatives will be working on the case to the exclusion of everything else and we will do our utmost to ensure your husband is returned safe and sound.'

I know, I know: 'skilled operatives' was stretching it a little, but I was hoping she hadn't noticed that, apart from me, they consisted of a small boy and a fat ex-genie dressed in bright yellow silk trousers.

She seemed reassured by my charm (in fairness, who wouldn't be) and got up to leave. As she walked to the door, something struck me – and it wasn't her forearm this time.

'Just one last question: have you talked to the police about this?'

'I reported it as soon as I found out he was missing, but they don't seem to be taking it too seriously. As there wasn't a ransom note and he's only been gone for a day, they're suggesting he might have just run off with someone else.' She hauled herself to her full height and bristled with indignation. 'As if!'

Frankly, if I was him, I'd be breaking all land-speed records to get as far away from this woman as was humanly (or porcinely) possible: she terrified me. 'Just out of curiosity, how long have you been married?'

She smiled proudly. 'Two hundred and thirty-seven years of wedded bliss last October.'

That stopped me in my tracks. 'He must be quite a man.' I couldn't think of anything else to say.

She nodded. 'And I, Mr Pigg, am quite a woman. I quickly put the police right on that particular theory of theirs, let me assure you, but I don't expect them to give it their full and undivided attention just yet – despite my best efforts to persuade them otherwise.'

I didn't have any doubts as to the effectiveness of her powers of persuasion; she'd already convinced me to take on her case – and against my better judgement too. It looked like I had a new client.

'OK, Mrs Claus, we'll probably need to check out your house and wherever your husband left from on the off chance there might be a clue as to what happened. Is there anyone else in the house at the moment – housekeeper, gardener, someone else who might know where your husband has gone?'

'Goodness no, apart from the local flight-control team and reindeer wranglers, there's just the two of us. All the rest of our employees are at our headquarters at the North Pole.'

'How many employees do you have up there?'

'Apart from the reindeer, we've got our admin staff and about one hundred elves. They're very diligent, you know.'

Elves! I'd probably have to talk to them as well; there was always the possibility that if this did turn out to be a kidnapping, someone there might be involved. Great! A trip to the North Pole in December: ice, snow, freezing temperatures and elves – and you know how much I dislike elves. They're pompous, arrogant, overbearing and talk in riddles – and that's just their good points.

'We'll need to interview everyone,' I said to her. 'Where's the nearest airport?'

'Let me take care of that,' she said. 'We have our own fleet of reindeer-powered luxury private sleighs that will take you straight to the facility.'

I wasn't sure how comfortable a private sleigh flight would be, but I imagined there wouldn't be much chance of an in-flight movie – or in-flight catering either. On a brighter note, I probably wouldn't be forced to sit between two Orcs and watch them fight over my peanuts. Every cloud, eh?

'I'll contact you when we need to go north, then,' I said to Mrs Claus.

She nodded in reply and turned to me as she went out of the door. 'Please don't let me down, Mr Pigg. Time is short and I don't have much of it to waste.' Although her tone was abrupt, I couldn't fail to notice the look of relief that skated quickly across her face before disappearing behind that stern mask once more. Maybe this wasn't a con job after all.

'We're on it,' I reassured her as she left the office.

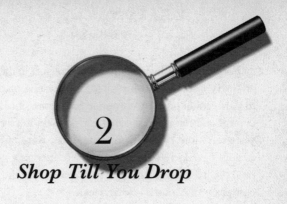

2

Shop Till You Drop

Seconds later – once they were sure she was gone – my two partners peered around the door. For those of you who don't know them, Basili was an ex-genie (don't ask) who I'd inherited after my last case and Jack Horner was an annoying small boy and wannabe detective with a tendency to always right and who had gotten me out of a tight spot or two recently. I hadn't the heart to sack either of them (yet).

'Is it OK to come in?' asked Jack nervously. I waved for them to enter and sit down.

'You two were a great help,' I said to them. 'Where were you when she had me pinned to the wall?'

Basili looked at me apologetically. 'Well, Mr Harry, you did seem to be having the situation under control and we were thinking it would be better if you perhaps spoke to the red woman on your own.'

For a moment I considered how dangling in the air while an angry woman used my throat as a resting place for her forearm could possibly constitute having the situation under control and then realised that my partners were cowards – yes, even more cowardly than me. They were just the kind of guys I could rely on when we were in a tight spot – rely on to beat a hasty retreat and leave me to face the music. A consensus of cowards – what a team.

'Well, it looks like we've got ourselves another case, so it's time to get to work. Jack, you need to start talking to other kids. Try to find out everything you can about Santa Claus. If anyone knows, kids will.' Jack nodded and raced out of the office, eager to be of assistance.

When Jack had disappeared down the stairs, Basili looked at me curiously. 'Why did you ask young Mr Jack to do this investigating? Surely he will return with the information that this Santa Claus is a jolly old man who is dressing in red, is being very happy and is bringing lots of nice things to them. This every child knows.'

'Exactly,' I replied. 'I just wanted him out of the way while I talked this case over with you. I didn't want him to hear what we were going to say.'

'With me? How can I be of assistance?'

'Because surely that story can't be true, can it? Think about it: how can one old man possibly deliver that many presents to that many houses all over the world in one night? It's not physically possible. At the very least it would take an army of Santas – and a fairly big army at that. If he was on his own and could get his sleigh to move fast enough to do the run in one night, both he and his reindeer would be vaporised in an instant. He'd never even get out of the hangar. He wouldn't be delivering too many toys then would he? Of course,' and I began to have that sinking feeling I knew only too well, 'there's always magic. As an ex-genie, and with your knowledge of things magical, is it possible that someone would be powerful enough to generate enough magic to actually allow him to do it?'

Basili thought for a moment and then shook his head. 'Even I would not have been capable of it. Such a power would go beyond the realms of magic. I have never heard of such a thing.'

'Exactly my thinking; now you can see why I didn't want Jack to hear. It would have destroyed his fantasy about Santa Claus and destroyed his Christmas. I certainly wouldn't want that on my conscience.'

'But, Mr Harry, it still begs the question: why did that red woman come to you? Even if what she has said is untrue, maybe her husband has still been kidnapped. She seemed to be most persuasive in that regard.'

I touched my neck gingerly. He had a point. 'Well, I suppose there's no harm in popping out to see the scene of the alleged crime, is there? It might give us a clue as to what's going on.'

Basili clapped his hands in excitement. 'A clue, a clue. Yes, that is what detectives do. We are finding clues and solving the mystery.'

He probably had an image of us arriving at the scene, walking around with a magnifying glass, picking up clues casually off the ground like we were picking fruit and having the mystery solved before lunch. I tried to bring him down gently. 'I don't think it's going to be that easy: there's still the possibility that Santa did a runner and will turn up later today looking embarrassed and begging for forgiveness – and if I was him I'd be doing some quality grovelling.' I stood up and put on my jacket. 'But before we do anything else, we need to go shopping.'

The ex-genie looked at me with a puzzled expression. 'Shopping, Mr Harry? At a time like this?'

'Yes, Basili, shopping. It may have escaped your notice, but as an apprentice detective, partner and potential undercover operative you are hardly a model of inconspicuousness at the present time.'

He carefully considered what he was wearing and acknowledged that I had a point. Flouncy yellow silk trousers that looked like he'd attached a pair of hot air balloons to his legs, an ornate shiny waistcoat that barely covered his chest and left most of his ample midriff exposed, and a pair of shoes that gave the impression they'd be more comfortable being piloted down a canal by a gondolier singing 'O Sole Mio' at the top of his voice. No, Basili needed new threads and fast, otherwise he'd be indefinitely confined to desk work.

The Ho Ho Ho Mystery

A thought struck me – desk work, now that's not a bad idea at all. It would certainly keep him out of the public eye and he could wear whatever selection of brightly coloured silks he possessed – and I probably wouldn't ever need to pay for lighting in my office again.

At the same time another more predatory thought (I have lots of those too) pointed out that if he did have as much money as he'd claimed then I needed to keep him sweet so I could use some of it to invest in the Third Pig Detective Agency like he'd promised. And don't get too upset by my seemingly mercenary attitude. The genie owed me. After all, it was me who had risked my precious hide by rescuing him from a very miffed Aladdin (and an even more miffed Edna) and making sure he wouldn't get caught up in that three wishes lark ever again. The least he could do in recompense was sub me some cash to buy some cool stuff.

I began clocking up my shopping list, all that kit I'd had to do without over the years: bugging devices, proper cameras, cool hi-tech surveillance equipment. With all that gear I could really outdo Red Riding Hood and consolidate my position as the foremost detective in town. All it was going to take was a bit of imagination and some shrewd investment at Gumshoes'R'Us and I was on my way.

'OK Basili, let's do it. Two hours from now you'll be stunningly sartorially elegant or my name's not Harry Pigg.'

*

Two hours from now the bottom had fallen out of my day.

'I'm sorry, sir, but that card is also being refused.' Danny Emperor, proprietor of Emperor's New Clothes Men's Emporium had run three of Basili's credit cards through the machine and all had been refused.

'Are you sure?' I asked, getting just a tad concerned. 'Can you try it one more time?'

Danny swiped the card once more and, once more, there was a high-pitched and (I thought) gleeful beeping as the system failed to validate it. I turned to the genie, who was becoming more dejected by the minute. He cut a forlorn – if somewhat conspicuous – figure, standing luminously among the racks of dark suits like a lighthouse in the middle of a bog. 'What's going on?' I asked him. 'Are you sure you were telling me the truth about all this money of yours?'

'Oh yes, Mr Harry,' he said glumly. 'As I told you, I had played the markets for many years while I was in the lamp. The return was, how shall I say, significant.'

'You could have fooled me,' I muttered to myself as Danny cut another of Basili's credit cards in two. As my dreams of a high-tech detective agency began to fade back into obscurity, a thought struck me. Reaching for my cellphone, I made a quick call to my lawyer, Sol Grundy (a man I keep very, very busy most of the time), and explained the situation to him. He told me he'd see what he could do and get back to me asap. If anyone could find out what was going on, he was the man. In the meantime all we could do was wait (and hope), surrounded by all the extra-large suits we were trying to buy.

Fortunately my lawyer works fast. Barely ten minutes had passed before he rang back.

'Sol,' I said, 'what's the story?'

'Not good, Harry.' Sol replied. 'Looks like your buddy has some problems. From what I've been able to find out, it looks as though Aladdin has had all his assets frozen, claiming that as they were acquired while your man was in his employ then, legally, they're Aladdin's. As of now, Basili has nothing. I know it sounds a bit high-handed and I'm not sure as to the legality of Aladdin's actions, but it's a grey area, so the courts will have to decide.'

'See what you can do, OK?' Aladdin was probably doing this out of sheer spite because we'd gotten one up on him. 'But watch out: that Aladdin is a slick operator.'

'Yes Harry, I'm aware of that. I wasn't born yesterday, you know.' Which was true, yesterday was Thursday. 'Oh, by the way, he's repossessed the lamp too.'

'He's more than welcome to it. It's worthless now.' Even the genie couldn't use it as a home now that he had no magic. He'd already bruised his big toe trying to get back into it through the spout. It was most definitely an ex-magic lamp. Then another awful thought struck me – it was clearly my day for them: if the genie couldn't get back into the lamp and had no money, then where was he going to live?

This was a question with only one possible answer: it looked like, for the foreseeable future, I was going to have a large, farting, silk-clad genie sleeping on my couch.

3
Wondering in a Winter Wonderland

The Claus house was so sweet and twee it made those candy cottages that dotted the Enchanted Forest look like outhouses. I could feel my teeth starting to decay and my arteries hardening just by looking at it. I'd probably die of a sugar overdose once I crossed the threshold. No matter what angle you looked at it from, it screamed Christmas in much the same way as Aladdin's mansion had screamed bad taste.

The house itself was a long, low log cabin – at least I think so. It was impossible to make out for sure, covered as it was from floor to roof in brightly coloured Christmas lights, which explained the bright glow in the sky we'd noticed as we drove over. These weren't just your usual strands of lights draped along the roof; oh no, there were rock bands that didn't have light shows as extravagant as what we were witnessing here. Rumour had it that Hubbard's Cubbard's lighting tech had spent six weeks studying these illuminations so he could get some good ideas for their next world tour. I couldn't say I blamed him; at any moment I expected a plane to land in the front garden, having mistaken the house for the approach to Grimmtown Airport. Even sunglasses wouldn't have been of any use here.

I could have sworn I even saw some people stretched out in the garden getting themselves a nice tan, but I couldn't be sure such was the assault on my eyes.

Seasonal ornaments covered the lawns. Reindeer jostled with Christmas gnomes; trees and snowmen seemed to be fighting for space with models of sleighs and Santas. It looked like a Christmas civil war had broken out and I had no idea who was actually winning. Even the corner of the swimming pool that I could see around the back of the house looked to have been covered with some sort of plastic ice on which mechanical rabbits, reindeer and snowmen skated happily away.

Snow covered the entire scene, giving it a little extra seasonal ambience – as if it really needed it. As we hadn't seen snow in Grimmtown for over five years, I used my powers of deduction to work out that it too, like everything else, was clearly fake.

Gingerly stepping around sunbathers and giant ornaments, I made my way to the door, pausing only to flick my fingers against a giant stalactite that hung from the eaves in front of me. Plastic too! I hammered on the reindeer-head door knocker, which lit up when I grabbed it and began singing 'Rudolph, the Red-nosed Reindeer'. It had gotten as far as 'Then one foggy Christmas Eve' before, to our relief, the door finally opened and Mrs Claus's familiar imposing figure peeked out. Just in case she wanted to exercise her forearm again I took a careful step back, but this time she seemed happier to see me – thankfully.

'Mr Pigg.' Then she saw Basili standing behind me. 'And your comedic sidekick, how nice.' There was an indignant snort from just over my left shoulder. 'It's good of you to come so soon. Please, come in.' She held the door open so we could enter.

Inside was just as tastefully decorated as outside. It seemed to be going for that ever-trendy neo-Lapland Rustic Charm look – as in pine everywhere. A mouth-watering aroma of mince pies emanated from a nearby kitchen. If the effect was to lull visitors into that warm Christmassy mood and leave them feeling good about themselves and everyone else, then it was very effective – until it came up against a cynical gumshoe like me. I was more of a 'Bah humbug' merchant when it came to Christmas.

Mrs Claus led us into a large living room dominated by a roaring fire. Gaudy red-and-white patterned socks hung from the pine mantelpiece and an enormous Christmas tree towered in one corner of the room. She indicated that we should sit in the comfortable-looking armchairs facing into the blazing inferno.

Once we were settled, I began. 'Has your husband contacted you?'

A quick shake of her head was the only response.

'Anyone else been in contact? A phone call or ransom note?'

Another shake of the head. Her lower lip began to tremble.

Please, no more waterworks, I thought to myself. *I didn't bring any wet gear.*

'Very odd,' I mused. 'I would have thought by now someone would have gotten in touch.' Of course, the fact that no one had contacted her gave credence to the police theory that Santa had done a runner – but I wasn't going to say that in front of the lady with the strongest forearms I'd ever seen. On the other hand, I had to be seen doing something to justify whatever fee I might get out of this case.

'Mrs Claus, do you mind if we have a look around? I'd particularly like to see where your husband left from yesterday. We might just spot something.' I have to confess that I couldn't see how it was possible for a sleigh and team of reindeer (whether they could fly or not) to actually leave the property; there just didn't seem to be any space available in the grounds to do so. Chances were that any vehicle trying to depart would end up colliding with a giant plastic snowman and crashing into a hill of artificial snow trailing streams of coloured lights behind it. Now there was a traffic accident I'd love to get the police report on!

After getting her consent, we went through the house looking for anything out of place, anything that might throw some light on what had happened. Let me tell you, there was so much Christmas junk around it was hard to tell what might constitute a clue. Everywhere we looked there was another tree laden down with tinsel or a sleigh hanging from the ceiling, and effigies of the man himself seemed to have been placed strategically in every room we entered. We certainly wouldn't have any difficulty identifying him; he was just like every picture you've ever seen: large, fat, jolly, dressed in red with a long white beard. I just hoped that we wouldn't be doing that identification as he lay on a slab in the morgue. That would certainly put a damper on Christmas – and would be more than a little difficult to explain to all the kids who were waiting expectantly for their presents.

Eventually we came to the conclusion that either the house had no clues whatsoever or else they were so successfully buried under mounds of festive tat we were never going to find them anyway. Even though Santa seemed to have taken his passport, some money and a suitcase of clothes (more red outfits, I assumed) with him when he'd left, Mrs Claus had advised that that was standard practice when he went to the North Pole. In fairness, I hadn't expected to find anything out of the ordinary, I was just covering all the bases.

4

Ground Control to Harry Pigg

The only thing we hadn't seen yet was the sleigh departure area and I asked if we could be taken there. Mrs Claus took us to a metal door – somewhat incongruous amidst the pine – and pressed a button on the wall beside it. It slid silently open and we were ushered into a tiny room, barely big enough to fit us all. Inside she pressed another button on a console and, after the door had closed again, we began to descend. Cool, I thought, we're on our way to some secret underground base.

I didn't realise how right I was. Once the lift had stopped and the doors opened, we stepped out on to a balcony overlooking a brightly lit, high-tech facility that bore no relation to the house constructed above it. Mrs Claus saw my look of astonishment and nodded.

'Yes, it's a bit different, isn't it? This is where the real business of Christmas is carried out – as well as at our North

Pole base, of course. What's above is only for show and to satisfy the expectations of the locals. After all, they do have certain preconceptions we must meet.'

I was tempted to tell her that these expectations could have been met with a lot more subtlety and taste, but bit my tongue before saying something I'd probably regret later. Instead I walked over to the edge of the balcony and looked down. Below me a large ramp curved up from the ground towards a flat ceiling, where it seemed to end abruptly. To one side a group of reindeer were being brushed down and led away to straw-lined stables. Over speakers that dotted the walls a loud voice was saying, 'Attention, attention, flight SCA219 has arrived safely from the North Pole. Reindeer have been unhitched and are being refuelled for the return flight, which will depart in approximately two hours. Please ensure all cargo has been loaded and safely strapped down. We do not want a repeat of the frisbee incident.'

I looked over at Mrs Claus and raised an inquisitive eyebrow.

She sighed heavily. 'One of our more infamous accidents. During a Christmas delivery back in the fifties a number of frisbees fell off the sleigh as we flew over a place called Roswell. We managed to gather them all back up before they could do too much damage, but unfortunately some of the larger ones – the ultra-giant luminous ones – were seen by a number of the locals. They caused quite a stir, you know.'

Now there was a perfect definition of the word 'understatement' – and she'd said the whole thing without any suggestion of irony.

'Ever since then we've made sure to keep all cargo securely fastened to avoid any further unpleasantness,' she concluded.

'I'm sure you have,' I said, trying to keep a straight face. 'Did anything else happen to fall off the sleigh at the same time?'

'Yes, we did lose two inflatable toy aliens as well. We never did find them that night. I've often wondered where they got to.'

Basili nudged me sharply in the side. 'Don't even be thinking about telling her, Mr Harry,' he whispered.

I nodded and bit my lip – but I was tempted. 'Mrs Claus, is it possible to talk to the air-traffic controller who was on duty when your husband disappeared? I'd like to get a better idea of the timings.'

'Yes, of course, and please call me Clarissa; Mrs Claus seems so formal, don't you think?'

She led us to a small control room that seemed to be wall-to-wall computers and consoles showing a bewildering series of numbers, radar displays and what presumably were flight paths. Sitting in front of them, speaking urgently into a large microphone was one very stressed air-traffic controller who seemed to be talking to seven different sleighs at once.

'Yes SCA74 you are clear to land. SCA42 please keep circling at your current height until you hear otherwise. No,

SCA107, I didn't get to record the Hubbard's Cubbard concert on TV last night for you. What's that, SCA92? Say again. Did I hear you correctly, you have a lame reindeer? Keep on this flight path and we'll divert you to the emergency runway. We'll have rescue teams standing by. Ground control out.' He pressed a button and sirens began to wail all around. 'Emergency, emergency; rescue teams to emergency runway. Repeat, rescue teams to emergency runway. We have a landing-gear problem on SCA92.'

There was a flurry of activity from down below as rescue teams in fire engines and ambulances raced out to the runway to await the arrival of the stricken sleigh. I turned to Mrs Claus. 'Does this kind of thing happen often?'

She shook her head. 'Not really – and, frankly, it's not much of an emergency either. All the reindeer has to do is keep his legs up when he lands and the others will bring him in safely. Our man here,' and she pointed at the harried controller, 'just likes to do things by the book.'

'Any chance I might have a quick word? I won't keep him too long.'

'Go right ahead.' She tapped the controller on the shoulder. 'Charles, this is Mr Pigg. He's investigating my husband's disappearance. He'd like to ask you some questions about the night he vanished.'

Charles nodded once but never took his eyes off the displays in front of him.

'OK, Charles. Can you tell us what happened?'

'Sure. Santa's private sleigh left here as scheduled at 21:00 hours. At 22:00 hours he contacted us to let us know that things were OK and that he was ascending to his cruising height. After that nothing, and he never arrived at Polar Central. That's all I know.'

'How long would the flight normally be?'

'About three hours, give or take.'

'And would it be unusual for Mr Claus to maintain radio silence for the duration?'

'It depends. It was a routine flight, so apart from an occasional update we might not hear from him until he was beginning his approach to Polar Central, so it wouldn't necessarily be a cause for concern. He does this run very regularly, you know.'

'I see, OK. Thanks, Charles.' He barely acknowledged me as he turned his attention back to his screens. I looked at Mrs Claus. 'Mrs Cl . . . I mean Clarissa, this is a most peculiar case. I can find no evidence of any wrongdoing here nor can I explain your husband's disappearance. Clearly he's missing, but I can't explain it. It is possible that I may be able to find out something by interviewing the staff at your North Pole base. How soon can you organise a flight for us since I'd like to start talking to them as soon as possible?'

'You can leave right now,' she said. 'We have a number of private sleighs – state of the art – that we keep on standby for any sudden or unexpected departures. They're very comfortable and should get you there in a matter of hours.'

Mrs Claus turned to Charles. 'Ask the ground crew to prep *Jingle Bells* for an immediate departure to Polar Central.'

'Yes, ma'am,' he replied and issued orders into a nearby radio.

As he spoke we were shepherded downstairs into an (admittedly very comfortable) departure lounge, where we were given heavy fur coats to wear – which didn't bode too well for the journey ahead. Once we were warmly wrapped up we were taken to the sleigh.

I have to confess at this point that I was expecting an open box with a hard wooden seat and large storage area; all sitting on top of two long, curved, metal skis with a team of smelly, flea-ridden reindeer attached to the front.

The reality was so very different.

A sleek red-and-white (of course) chassis, like a giant covered bobsleigh, rested on huge, sturdy-looking skis. To my relief there was no sign of outside seats so it looked as though we'd be inside – and warm, I hoped. Naturally it wasn't all high-tech. I'd been expecting something like rocket-powered engines, so I was a tad disappointed to see a team of twelve reindeer being hooked up to the front of the sleigh, but at least they looked the part too: sleek, strong and very healthy looking. I just wasn't too sure they'd manage to get the sleigh off the ground.

Mrs Claus saw my look of uncertainty and quickly reassured me, 'They're Class Two reindeer; some low-level raw magic and power. Don't worry; they'll get us there without difficulty.'

Magic: I knew there'd be magic involved somewhere. I didn't share her confidence. Magic and me just didn't mix. If something was going to go wrong with this craft, chances were it would be when I was travelling in it.

Slowly and with a large degree of caution I approached the sleigh. As I did, a door in the side slid quietly open, revealing a luxurious interior. Large, comfortable-looking seats lined the walls and a plush carpet covered the floor. No prizes for guessing the colour scheme. Hey, maybe this wouldn't be too bad after all.

One of the ground crew approached. 'Everyone inside please, we depart in five minutes.'

We all entered and quickly strapped ourselves into the seats. I sank into mine and it surrounded me like I was in a hot bath. This was the life. If I didn't know better I'd have thought I was in someone's living room. Across from me Basili struggled with his seat belt and looked anxiously at me. I gave him a reassuring smile, but he didn't seem too convinced. Maybe he didn't like flying either – which was strange, considering he used to be a genie and spent most of the time when he popped out of his lamp hanging in the air with smoke for legs. I hoped for his sake we'd have an uneventful flight.

Behind me Mrs Claus was talking to our in-flight steward and asking him to organise drinks and something to eat as soon as we were airborne. As he walked back to the galley, there was a sudden jolt and the sleigh began to move forward along the ramp. As we began to pick up speed, I noticed – somewhat nervously – that we were racing up the ramp towards the ceiling I'd seen earlier. The sleigh got faster and faster as we approached the blank wall ahead.

'Shouldn't there be a door or something?' I shouted over my shoulder to Mrs Claus, who was lying back with her eyes closed, seemingly blissfully unaware of our imminent collision.

'Don't worry, Mr Pigg. I'm sure the pilot knows what he's doing.'

Outside, the scenery was passing by in a blur as the reindeer picked up speed, apparently oblivious to their impending doom.

The ceiling got closer and closer and I got more and more scared. 'Ohmigod, we're all gonna die; we're all gonna die; WE'RE ALL GONNA DIIIIAAAARGH.' As I screamed in terror at our imminent collision with the ceiling, it suddenly split in two and the sleigh shot out through the opening. Through the window I got a blurred glimpse of the swimming pool parting on either side as we came up through it. Seconds later we'd left the ground behind us and hurtled into the night sky.

'There,' came a sleepy voice from behind me. 'I told you he knew what he was doing.'

34

5

And Pigs Might Fly

I sank back in my seat, sweating . . . well, um, like a pig actually. I was close to hyperventilating and tried to get my breathing under control before I passed out. Across the aisle Basili was studying me with interest, seemingly oblivious to what just happened.

'You are well, Mr Harry?' he asked.

'I'll live,' I gasped. 'But I don't think I'll be able to cope with any more scares like that.'

Behind me, a gentle snoring sound suggested Mrs Claus was far less worried than either of us.

'I am sure there will be no more incidents until after we are arriving at our destination.' Basili unfastened his belt – which was clearly making him uncomfortable – let his seat back and closed his eyes. Seconds later he too was snoring, but much louder than the ladylike trilling from Mrs Claus. Great: snoring in stereo for the rest of the trip! I wondered if there was an in-flight movie; I could certainly do with some distraction.

Unfortunately, it looked as though the nearest I was going to get to in-flight entertainment was looking out of the window. Mind you, judging by the speed at which the clouds passed by it seemed that the reindeer were moving at quite a clip. Maybe there was some germ of truth in what Mrs Claus had told me. If these were Class Two animals, I wondered how fast Class One reindeer could go. Idly musing on thoughts like this (and because I had nothing else to do – the current case proving to be completely devoid of any leads), I eventually sank into a light doze.

A loud blaring brought me to my senses. The captain was shouting at us through the intercom. 'Attention, passengers. Ground control has detected another craft approaching us at speed. We have as yet been unable to make contact with them. Please return to your seats and ensure your seat belts are securely fastened while we establish what is going on. Thank you.'

Just as he finished there was a loud thud on the side of the sleigh as something made heavy contact. The impact caused the sleigh to lurch wildly and turn on its side. Before I could grab on to anything, I slid across the floor and smashed into the cabin door. Showing scant regard for safety regulations and quality construction, it swung open and I dropped out of the sleigh into the freezing night.

I felt a trotter bang off something as I fell. Using whatever innate survival instincts I possessed (I certainly wasn't doing this by design – trust me), my other trotter swung around and clung desperately to one of the sleigh's landing skis. The sleigh careened wildly as it was hit again and I just managed to keep my grip. Almost immediately, Basili's semi-conscious body fell out of the cabin above and plummeted past me. Using the same innate sense of self-preservation I'd used, his arms were stretched out trying to grab on to anything that might save him. Unfortunately for me, he wasn't quite as good at it as I was. Instead of grabbing the ski, he wrapped an arm around my legs and clutched them tightly.

I tried to look down at the ex-genie dangling from my legs. 'Basili,' I shouted, trying to be heard over the wind, 'can you climb up my body and grab on to a ski?'

'I do not think so, Mr Harry. I am barely feeling my hands. It is a most unusual and unpleasant sensation. Perhaps if I am letting go, you may be able to climb back in.'

'Not an option, Basili,' I muttered through gritted teeth. 'We need to come up with something else – and quickly.'

'Trust me, Mr Harry,' came the strained voice from below. 'I am thinking as fast as I can.'

As I gamely struggled for inspiration, there came a voice from above asking what was, in the circumstances, possibly the most idiotic question I'd ever heard.

'Are you two gentlemen OK?' asked Mrs Claus, peering down from the open door.

'Not really. Now if you would be so kind as to find something we can grab on to before we end up trying to fly of our own accord, we'd be really grateful.'

'One moment, I'll see what I can do.' Her head disappeared back into the sleigh before I could point out that we really didn't have the luxury of a moment to spare.

'Hold on, Basili,' I roared down to the genie. 'Help may be on its way.' As I did so, my trotters began to slip away from the skis. Frantically, I tried to hold on, but the strain was too much. My trotters protested at what they were being asked to do – they didn't seem to think it was fair. Inch by inch they began to slide apart. I wasn't going to manage it.

Just as I was about to give way, Mrs Claus shouted down at us again. 'Here, grab on to this.' Something snaked past my shoulder and I grabbed on to a thick rope and held on to it as if my life depended on it (which it did).

I was just thanking my lucky stars, lucky rabbit's foot, lucky anything-else-lucky-I-had-in-my-possession when the big, ugly, hob-nailed boot of fate stamped down on me one more time. The sleigh skewed wildly as our attackers hit it once again. There was a scream and I saw a blur of red as something large fell past me. There was an almighty tug on my legs as if someone had attached something heavy – like, say, a truck – to them.

Whatever chance I had of hanging on while Basili dangled from my legs had disappeared when Mrs Claus added her ample frame to the equation. Now, I could feel the rope sliding through my trotters as my arms finally gave up, shouted surrender and lay down their weapons. I didn't know how long the rope was, but from the speed I slid down along it I didn't think there was much more left to hold on to. This was it; this was the end.

6

The Soft Shoe Slingshot

O r was it?

I didn't plummet down through the inky blackness and end up an unpleasant mess on the ground below (as I'd not unreasonably expected) but landed instead on something hard and metallic. Behind me I could hear Basili crying, 'Thank the gods', and, behind him again, Mrs Claus was just crying. I didn't even bother trying to work out what had happened; I just lay where I was and breathed a heavy sigh of relief. From the speed of the wind across my face it seemed like we were on something that was moving fast – but what? When the surface underneath me lurched sharply and I saw us move towards the sleigh we'd just fallen from, I knew exactly where we were.

Were we safe? Hell, no!

Were we in a better position than before? Marginally – in the sense that we weren't hanging off each other and facing certain death.

Where exactly were we? We'd fallen on to the roof of the sleigh that had been attacking us!

Was that better? Only if it flew in a straight line.

I turned to my companions and broke the good news to them. From what I could see of their expressions they were less than gruntled too. Clearly they shared my opinion of our predicament.

'Is there any way we can climb down and get into this sleigh?' bellowed Mrs Claus.

'I doubt it,' I shouted back, trying to make myself heard over the howling wind. 'If we let go of what we're holding, we'll be blown off. More to the point, do you really want to climb into a sleigh full of people who have been trying to kill us for the past ten minutes?'

'Good point. So what do we do now?'

The obvious answer (if any solution to this predicament could be called obvious) would be to get back to our own sleigh and try to escape from our attackers. Yeah, easy really; all we had to do was jump from one sleigh to another while travelling at great speed thousands of feet in the air. Easy!

Of course, I had no idea where our sleigh was. If our pilot had any sense he was flying as far from our attackers as possible to preserve his hide. It's what I'd have done.

But he proved me wrong. There was a drumming sound from above and a flurry of hooves narrowly missed my head. I looked up and saw our sleigh hovering inches above me.

Through the cockpit window our pilot was waving madly at us, urging us to get back in.

I didn't need a formal invitation. I grabbed the ski that was hanging above me and pulled myself up and back into the passenger section. Seconds later, the other two fell in on top of me and we lay on the floor gasping for breath.

'No time,' I urged. 'We need to get strapped in now. I don't know about you two, but I certainly wouldn't care for a repeat of that little adventure.'

For big people they could move fast when they wanted. Both of them were in their seats and buckled before I'd even stood back up. Once I was secure I grabbed the armrests and held on as if my life depended on it – which, when you think about it, it did. There was no way I was falling out of that door again. No thank you very much.

Mrs Claus spoke to the pilot and the gist of the long conversation was 'Get us the hell out of here as fast as you can.' I couldn't make out all of his reply but I did pick up the words 'faster than us' and 'reindeer getting tired'. No matter how I juggled the phrases in my head, I couldn't make them into a sentence that didn't mean bad news for us.

'Are we in trouble?' I asked.

'You mean worse trouble than we're already in? Marginally. The pilot doesn't think he can get away; the reindeer are tiring and we've taken a fair bit of damage.'

'But that other sleigh must be having problems too. Surely in all the battering it gave us, it must have taken a dent or two? What about its reindeer? They must be tired too.'

'Ah, but I'm told that their sleigh is one of those new-fangled jet-powered ones. No reindeer to tire, I'm afraid. Unless they run out of fuel soon, we don't stand a chance.'

Mrs Claus waved frantically in the direction of the still-open door. 'Brace yourselves, here they come again.'

'Sod this for a game of skittles,' I exclaimed, partly in frustration but mostly in anger. I wasn't sure if there was anything I could do but I wasn't just going to sit there and wait for us to fall out of the sky. I unbuckled my seat belt and stood up carefully – ever mindful of the gaping hole where the door used to be. Looking around the cabin, I saw another door in the rear wall. 'What's in there?' I asked.

'Just some light luggage for me, some raw materials for the toy factory and other bits and pieces. Nothing important. Why do you ask?' said Mrs Claus.

I scrambled back and pulled the door open. 'Because I'm fed up with waiting to be bumped out of the sky. I'm going to try to fight back. There might be nothing I can do but I'll feel a whole heap better.'

I examined the contents of the luggage area. Mrs Claus was right. There didn't seem to be much that I could use as a weapon. Large crates were stacked neatly and fastened to the walls. Just in front of them was a mountain of suitcases that filled the rest of room. 'Light luggage' indeed. If this was what she took for an overnight trip to the North Pole,

I shuddered to think what she might need for a two-week vacation.

Nope, nothing useful here. I banged my fist against the door in frustration and, just as I was about to give up, a thought struck me.

Suitcases!

I grabbed a medium-sized one and hefted it. Heavy – but I could still carry it. Maybe . . . just maybe.

I dragged it across the floor towards the open door. Mrs Claus saw me. 'Hey, what are you doing with that suitcase? It's mine.' I chose to ignore her. At the door I clung to the frame and waited. In the distance I could see the large dark shape of the jet sleigh moving rapidly in our direction once more.

I lifted the case and swung it gently once or twice to get the balance right. The sleigh grew bigger as it neared our ailing craft. 'Strap yourselves in guys; we're in for some chop,' came the captain's voice over the intercom. I ignored him; I was through with strapping myself in.

The dark outline of the approaching sleigh was completely blocking out what little starlight there was. I waited for my opportunity and, with what little strength I had left, I flung the suitcase out of the door and straight at it. It made a satisfying contact and I heard the engine tone change from a low growl to a high-pitched and strangled whine – the kind of sound that suggested I had done some damage. I watched the sleigh began to spin wildly over and over like a nuclear-powered spinning top. Whoever was in it was going to be very sick, very soon. Whirling madly, it careened wildly away from us, out of control and no longer a threat.

Of course, there was a knock-on effect too (there always is). As the turbine shredded the suitcase, it flung bits of shoes in all directions – like leather machine-gun bullets. There was a shriek of anguish from behind me. It sounded like Mrs Claus had been hit by the shrapnel.

How wrong I was.

'My Manolos,' she wailed. 'You've destroyed my Manolos.'

Manolos? What were Manolos? I looked at Basili. Maybe he knew what she was talking about.

'I think she is most unhappy that the suitcase you have ejected from our craft was full of her very expensive shoes.'

Oh, was that all? So it wasn't serious then, although from the sound of her you'd think someone had just died. She hadn't cried like that when we were in danger. Women!

7

Ice Station Santa

The North Pole was cold. No, that's an understatement: ice cream is cold, beer is cold; this was a whole new sensation that the word *cold* had only a passing acquaintance with. This was extremities turning blue cold, struggling to breathe cold and, most of all, impossible to walk on sheet ice with trotters cold. As soon as I stepped out of what was left of our battered sleigh, I wanted to race right back inside, huddle under a cosy blanket and wait until spring. At least now I knew why we'd been given all that warm gear back in Grimmtown.

We walked – well, slid might be more accurate – towards a small welcoming committee. Four people stood outside the arrivals area, clearly waiting for us. When we were near enough for them to approach without landing on their backsides the smallest of the group, a very pleasant and worried-looking woman, rushed forward and hugged Mrs Claus tightly.

'Oh, Clarissa,' she wept. 'I'm so glad you're safe. When we heard the news we feared the worst.'

Mrs Claus pushed her away gently. 'It's all right, Mary. It wasn't too pleasant, but we're here now and we're OK.'

'Wasn't too pleasant!' That was like saying Red Riding Hood wasn't too irritating – it made no effort to describe exactly how terrifying our experience had been. Before I could tell everyone how I had saved us all from certain death, I caught the warning look Mrs C was giving me – better not say too much until we knew exactly who was listening. I still had no idea what was going on but despite my initial doubts there was clearly a mystery to be solved here – and with my usual magnetic attraction to such mysteries, it was one of those that was hell-bent on putting my delicate hide in as much danger as possible.

No change there, then.

As I mused on how consistently unlucky I was in my choice of clients, I became aware that Mrs C (that's what I was calling her now – it seemed catchier than Mrs Claus and I was still nervous about calling her Clarissa) was trying to make introductions. She waved at the woman first. 'This is Mary; she runs the show at the North Pole while we're in Grimmtown. You'll find she is a most capable administrator and can probably tell you anything you want to know about what goes on here.'

Mary grasped my trotter in a firm, welcoming handshake. 'Very pleased to meet you, Mr Pigg. I've heard a lot about you.'

'Glad to meet you too, Mary. Mary um . . . ?' I replied, trying to get her surname.

'Mary,' she said.

'Mary?' Once more with feeling.

'Mary.' And again.

'Ah,' Mrs C interrupted. 'There seems to be some confusion here.'

You have no idea, I thought.

'This is Mary Mary. She's a bit contrary, hence the difficulty. We originally hired her to look after our gardens here, but she was so good she eventually became our facility manager.'

They had gardens here? What grew in them? Icicles?

'Ah,' I said, 'I see.' Although I wasn't sure I saw at all.

'And these are our heads of toy manufacturing.' She indicated the three elves who had accompanied Mary. 'This is Carigrant, head of Trad Toys.' The first of the elves gave me a weak, dismissive half-wave. 'And this is Gladaerial, head of Tech Toys.' Again, another superior, flippant acknowledgement. 'And finally, this is Gilgrisum, head of R&D.' Gilgrisum raised an eyebrow a fraction of an inch, which I assumed was the elven equivalent of rushing over to me, hugging me tightly and roaring 'Great to meet you' in my ear.

Mrs Claus continued, 'They will arrange for any interviews you might want to have with the workers.'

In truth, I didn't *want* to interview any elves; it was more a case of having to. For reasons outlined before, I disliked elves intensely. It was hard to trust a race who spent most of their time being obsessed with personal hygiene and looking at themselves in mirrors. And I wasn't too enamoured with the way they spoke either.

As if he could read my thoughts, 'A detective arrives; mysteries will be solved this night,' said Carigrant, right on cue.

See what I mean. Why not just say it plainly: Harry Pigg is here; all our problems are over. This genius detective will have things wrapped up before you can say something long-winded and pretentious.

'How many elves do you have working here?'

'One hundred,' said Mary Mary promptly.

Great – one hundred gibberish interviews. I wondered if it was possible to get an elvish interpreter – although I imagined after two days in the job they'd be quite insane. As jobs go, I'd rate it up there with Orc etiquette coach and wolf dentistry. Still, this is why I get paid the big bucks (or, as is more usual, small bucks paid in instalments or replaced by a basket of fruit or an IOU – usually the last).

It was time to get down to business. I addressed everyone, 'Right, we're not sure what has happened to Mr Claus – I mean, Santa. It's quite likely he's been kidnapped, so someone here may know something about it. I'll be talking to everyone so please make sure your teams know this. I'd also appreciate it if you would ask them to be as candid as possible. The more information we have, the better. It may be just one small detail that they might even consider unimportant, but it could be crucial.'

From the looks on their faces, they seemed to take my statement with a degree of disbelief, as if I was impugning the integrity of their workforce. Who, me?

I continued, 'We'll also need some place to work out of for the duration.'

Mrs C nodded. 'I'll make sure you have somewhere suitable. Mary, please organise a room for Mr Pigg.' Mary nodded and scurried off, followed a few moments later by the elves – who didn't scurry, they were far too dignified. They moved gracefully over the frozen surface as if it was made of asphalt. Typical – even on ice they looked elegant.

Behind me I heard a strange rattling noise. Too cold for snakes, I thought as I turned to investigate. It was Basili's teeth hammering out a very impressive drum solo he was so cold. 'P . . . p . . . perhaps we g . . . g . . . go inside now, p . . . p . . . please. It is m . . . m . . . m . . . most c . . . c . . . cold out here.' He wasn't used to temperatures like this. When he was attached to his lamp, he probably spent his time being washed up on warm sunny beaches and being summoned into bright sunlight to do as his latest master might bid – or at least that's how I imagined it. Poor beggar probably only saw ice when he added it to his margarita after settling down in his lamp of an evening after a hard day's magic.

'A good idea,' I said. 'It is a bit chilly out here.' My talent for understatement is unsurpassed.

Minutes later we were in – oh joy – a warm and welcoming reception area. A Christmas theme was (inevitably) the order of the day, except that here large images of the main man dominated. A huge picture that stretched from floor to ceiling hung behind the reception desk and large red statues of Santa dotted around the room were hard to miss. I wondered if there might be some over-compensation issues here – on top of everything else – but I was smart enough to just nod my head maniacally and comment on how tasteful the décor was. Basili gave me an incredulous look, but I managed to nudge him sharply in the side before he could say anything that might reflect badly on me.

Mary Mary approached us and ushered us into a slightly more tastefully decorated meeting room. A tinny 'Santa Claus Is Coming to Town' was being piped in to set the atmosphere. Not this year, I thought, unless I suddenly had a major breakthrough in the case.

'You can use this room for the duration of your stay,' said Mary Mary. 'Everyone has been instructed to cooperate fully with your investigation. If you need anything else, don't hesitate to contact me.'

'Thank you very much,' I said. 'Apart from the elves, is there anyone else here I should be talking to?'

Mary Mary thought for a moment. 'Well, there's Rudolph. He is quite close to Santa. He might be able to help.'

'Right then, we'll need to speak to him too. Can you set it up for us?'

Mary Mary shifted uncomfortably. 'Well, you don't really talk to Rudolph; you listen. He's got quite a strong personality.' By that I presumed she meant he was an arrogant, superior reindeer with an attitude problem. That was fine; it wouldn't be the first time I'd experienced that.

'Why don't you let me worry about that?' I said. 'I'm sure he'll talk to us. In fact, why don't we get him in here as our first interviewee?'

'Oh goodness, no,' Mary Mary exclaimed. 'He doesn't do house calls. You'll have to make an appointment to see him. He's very busy, you know.'

I wasn't having any of that. 'I doubt it very much. I imagine the only time he's busy is on Christmas Eve when he does his "Rudolph with your nose so bright" routine at the front of the sleigh. Let's go and see him now.' I strode purposefully out of the office and stopped when I realised I had no idea where I was going. Somewhat abashed, I waited for the others to join me.

'OK, where does Rudolph hang out when he's not on sleigh duty?' I asked.

'His rooms are this way.' Mary Mary pointed down a nearby corridor. 'But I don't think he'll see you.'

'Oh, I beg to differ.' Determination writ large on my face, I marched down the corridor. Seconds later I stood outside a heavy wooden door. A large sign surrounded by flashing fairy lights read: 'Rudolph. Unavailable from 24th December to 26th December. Any other time by appointment only.'

'Who does he think he is?' I muttered as I flung the door open and walked in. Inside, a very nervous gnome sat at a small desk, guarding a set of double doors at the far side of a small lobby. When he saw us, he stood up and brandished a pen angrily in our direction.

'You can't go in there,' he squeaked. 'You don't have an appointment.'

'Wrong. I can, I do and I will.' I walked past him towards the double doors.

In fairness to him he tried to stop me, but I brushed him aside, swung the doors open and stopped abruptly, jaw hitting the ground. I wasn't sure what I'd expected to see, perhaps a plush office, ornate mahogany desk, comfortable leather chairs, expensive carpet and lots of plants; I certainly didn't expect . . . well, the first thing that caught my eye was the reindeer.

Instead of a flea-ridden, hay-chomping animal resting up in a straw-lined stable getting ready for his big night, I got a sleek reindeer draped across a divan, clad in a red dressing gown and matching silk pyjamas. An elf stood on either side of him; one dropping grapes into his upturned mouth while the other waved a large feather over his head – presumably to cool him down. On a small table beside him a large cigar burned away in an ornate ashtray.

As we entered Rudolph looked up sharply, clearly annoyed at the unexpected intrusion.

'Who the hell are you and what are you doing in here uninvited? Do you know who I am?' His voice had an upper-class twang that was purely for effect. It sounded like he'd practised it every day until he got it just right and used it to intimidate people. Well, he was intimidating the wrong person here. I walked straight up to where he was lying and stuck my snout into his face.

'I'm the guy who's been asked to find out what happened to your boss. I invited myself and, yes, not only do I know who you are but I don't really care. Any more questions?' I stood there staring into his eyes, willing myself not to blink first. We continued to glare at each other, each waiting for the other to crack. He didn't realise he was up against the best; I could outstare a basilisk. This time, however, I thought I'd met my match as he glared at me, gaze unwavering, his brown eyes drilling into mine, challenging me. Just as my eyes began to water over (please don't blink, Harry; please don't blink), Rudolph capitulated, clearly realising who was boss (or maybe he just had to close his eyes) and turned his face away. When I was sure he couldn't see me I blinked furiously to relieve my aching peepers. Pig 1, reindeer 0.

'Good,' I said. 'Now that we've gotten that out of the way, I'd like to ask you some questions.'

Rudolph was still trying to gain the upper hand. 'I'm somewhat busy at the moment; if you'd care to make an appointment I'm sure I can squeeze you in early next week.'

I'd had enough. I grabbed him by the silk lapels and pulled him up so he was staring once more into my face. This time I wasn't interested in a staring contest. 'Listen, antler boy, I don't know who you think you are but I don't have time for this upper-class twit-of-the-year nonsense. Your boss's wife has asked me to find him and I'm going to do that to the best of my ability. As part of that investigation I need to talk to you and we are going to do that right now. Are you OK with that, or do I have to incentivise you in some way?' I flicked my head casually towards Basili, who was standing nervously in the door. Now I knew that, as an enforcer, Basili was about as useful as a snowman stoking a furnace but Rudolph didn't and, in fairness, Basili did look the part – up to a point.

Rudolph looked at Basili, looked back at me, looked at Basili again and made up his mind. 'OK, let's talk.' As he did so, I noticed something very strange happen to his nose: it began to glow slightly, giving off a reddish light that cast his face in shadow.

'Does that happen often?' I said, fascinated.

'Usually when I get emotional,' Rudolph replied. 'The more emotional I get, the stronger the light becomes. It's what sets me apart from the others.'

I was tempted to point out that dressing in red silk pyjamas and being fed grapes probably set him apart from the others too, but I didn't; sometimes I'm just too nice.

'So you really do lead the sleigh on Christmas Eve then?'

Rudolph nodded. 'Yes, it can get very foggy, you know. That's when I'm needed most. But they have to make me very angry if it's to be really effective.'

'What do they do, deprive you of elocution classes?'

Sarcasm was completely lost on him. 'No, they just put me in with the rest of the reindeer for a week. That really bugs me: no dress sense, bad table manners and an unhealthy fascination with reality TV. I tell you, it would make anyone mad, let alone someone of my obvious refinement.'

I almost felt for him. Maybe it would have been easier just to take his jimmies and grapes away. That'd probably do the trick without the need to inflict him upon the other unfortunate reindeer. Why should they have to suffer too? That was just cruel and unusual. And speaking of cruel and unusual, now I had to try to interview this twit.

I went through all the usual questions and received all the usual answers until I came to the 'Any reason why anyone might want to kidnap Santa?' one. Although he shook his head and said he couldn't think of any, there was that same hint of evasion I thought I'd detected with Mrs C. Now I was beginning to get the feeling that there was more going on here than I'd previously thought. Despite their denials, both Mrs C and Rudolph had given the distinct impression that they knew more than they were letting on. But what was it? And how did it relate to the case? More questions; fewer answers. Maybe the elves might be able to tell us something – although I doubted it very much.

Telling Rudolph not to make any travel plans as we'd probably need to speak to him again, we left and made our way back to our interview room.

'What a clown,' I said to Basili. 'And now we get to talk to elves.'

Despite my own reservations, Basili seemed to be looking forward to the next set of interviews (ah, the enthusiasm of the newly minted detective!).

8

I Am Not Spock

'Very well then,' Basili said, rubbing his hands – he was really getting into this – 'it is time to be talking to some elven peoples.'

'Well, that could be a bit of a misnomer; it's more like we'll look at them blankly while their mouths make noises that could perhaps be construed as talking, then we'll try to make some sense of whatever we think they've just said. And we'll have to do this one hundred times,' I replied. 'Just so as you know, this will be like pulling teeth, only more painful. I suspect that by the end of the day your ears will be bleeding and you'll wish you were back with Aladdin.'

'Oh, Mr Harry, I do not think so. Surely nothing could be worse than spending year after year stuck in that lamp waiting to grant one final wish.' He did have a point there, although it was probably a photo-finish to decide which was worse.

After the seventh interview, I suspected he was having a change of mind. I could see his eyes were glazing over and a thin trail of drool trickled from the corner of his mouth. He was rapidly losing his sanity, his grip on reality and his will to live – and we had another ninety-three elves to talk to! He buried his head in his hands and wailed mournfully. 'Oh, Mr Harry, I do not know how much more of this I am taking. I am failing to comprehend any word these elvish folk are speaking.'

I understood his plight; I was hovering on the brink of complete mental breakdown too. My grasp of what was real – already eroded by Christmas decoration overdose and my conversation with Rudolph – was now being washed away in a sea of double talk and nonsense. Just to give you an example:

Conversation One:

Question: When did you last see Mr Claus?

Answer: The gentleman in red was perambulating the environs some weeks hence but has not been in attendance at the child's plaything fabrication facility for some thirty-six planetary rotations.

Conversation Two:

Question: Are you aware of any reason why someone might want to harm Mr Claus?

Answer: Gentleness is his path; harm will not be the stone upon which he trips.

The Ho Ho Ho Mystery

If I was to interpret what we were being told correctly, Santa hadn't been seen at the North Pole since his last visit some thirty-six days earlier and no one knew of any reason why anyone might want to do him harm. At least, that's what I think they were telling me. I wasn't sure the other ninety-three interviews would change that.

Or would they?

Candidate eighty-six set all kinds of alarm bells ringing. His story was the same as all the others, but when he'd left the room I told Basili we needed to carry out further investigations into that particular elf.

'Why so, Mr Harry?' he asked.

'Well, did you notice anything strange about him?'

'No, I was so concentrating on staying awake that I did not fully take in what he was talking about.'

'No, Basili,' I said. 'It's not what he was saying; he sounded just the same as all the others. Did you not notice anything about his personal grooming?'

Basili raised an eyebrow.

It looked like it was time for elves 101. 'Let me list them for you: he was unshaven, his hair was greasy (and not tied back in an ever so look-at-me-I'm-cool ponytail), his clothes weren't ironed and, most importantly, he had BO.'

'So?' Basili was even more confused.

'So, when have you ever seen an elf that wasn't immaculately turned out? They fancy themselves as style icons (if you like Lincoln green tights and pointy boots, that is) and are obsessed with personal hygiene. I think it's fair to say elf number eighty-six is a ringer and a badly prepared ringer at that. He really should have washed himself, or at least applied some deodorant.' I stood up, excitement building now that we had a lead at long last. 'Let's see what we can find out about him.'

'Why don't we take him down to the station, let the boys be sorting him out?' Basili was hopping up and down enthusiastically (and let me tell you it wasn't a pretty sight). I wondered what kind of TV shows he'd been watching while stuck in the lamp.

'That's not how things are done,' I said – although, it being elves, the idea did have some merit. 'Anyway, we don't want to let him know we're on to him. The best thing to do is keep a discreet eye on him and see what he does; or maybe,' a thought had just struck me, 'we can try to get close to him and see if he'll let anything slip. He certainly doesn't strike me as being too bright.'

'Yes, but how? We are much too big and, anyway, you are a pig. Even he would be spotting the attempt at deception.' Basili was right. Apart from the three elves we'd met when we arrived, all the others were northern elves and much smaller than their southern cousins. In fact, they were just like the elves you've seen depicted in those cheerful Christmas cards showing Santa's workshop – just a lot less cheerful and a lot more pompous in reality. Even the dimmest of elves would have no difficulty seeing through whatever disguise we might adopt. No, we needed someone else; someone smaller; someone with the brass neck to be able to pull a deception like this off.

I smiled broadly. 'Basili, I think I have a plan.'

'No way! There is no way on this planet that I'm wearing those things.' Jack Horner was indignant. He flung the fake ears we'd given him on the ground. 'They're the most idiotic things I've ever seen. They look like they were made out of a cereal box.'

There's ingratitude for you. With Mrs C's help, we'd managed to fly him at inordinate expense to a place most children would give both arms to visit and all he had to do in return was dress up as an elf for a few minutes. Sometimes I just don't understand children.

I tried to placate him. 'Jack, Jack, take it easy. We need someone to mingle with the elves and find out what number eighty-six is up to. That someone has to be fearless, able to think on his feet and be brave in the face of certain danger.' OK, I was laying it on with a trowel, but I knew how to get to him. 'When I started to draw up a list of suitable candidates only one name sprang to mind. I still remember how you risked certain death to rescue me from Edna's.'

Jack preened himself. I could see my hyperbole was working. 'You know, I might just be the answer to your prayers,' he said. 'But there's still no way I'm wearing those stupid cardboard ears. Get me something that looks real and I'll think about it.'

Result!

I grinned happily. 'Looks like the team are all together and hot on the trail once more.'

'Yep,' replied Jack. 'Now we just need to find some fake ears.'

'We're in the biggest toy-manufacturing facility in the world; just how difficult do you think it's going to be?'

Very, as it turned out.

Play-Elf outfits were so last year that no one wanted them any more. All available stock had been recycled as Robin Hood costumes, but as Sherwood Forest's most famous inhabitant wasn't noted for having pointy ears, they had all been melted down and remoulded into Hubbard's Cubbard action figures (and they weren't selling too well either; rock bands aren't in great demand as toys). We had scoured workshops, storage bins and were rummaging through a disused warehouse full of obsolete toys when Jack shouted, 'Would this work?' and waved a large, if somewhat battered crate at us. We gathered around to see what he'd found.

I blew years of accumulated dust off the top of the box and read the contents. 'Yes, this might just do the trick.' Opening it, I took out a pair of black pants and a dark blue top. Throwing them to one side, I continued to search. 'So far, so good,' I murmured. 'Now somewhere in here there should be . . . aha, got you.'

Very carefully, I removed what looked like two dead pink slugs and carefully unrolled them in my hand. 'I haven't seen one of these in years. They were all the rage in the sixties.'

Beside me, Jack picked up the cover of the box and studied it.

'What's logic?' he asked. Before I could answer he continued, 'What's a phaser?' and, barely pausing for breath, 'Who's Mr Spock? He looks kinda weird.' He handed me the box and I read it:

> Now you too can be a master of logic.
> Be the envy of your friends as you stun them with your Vulcan nerve pinch.
> Beam up this box and be Mr Spock.
> Note: the phaser is a toy and will not disintegrate either humans or aliens (batteries not included).

A picture of one of science fiction's most famous pointy-eared non-humans adorned the cover.

'This guy was one of the most famous TV aliens of all time but, most importantly,' I held up the two unrolled pink things, 'he had pointy ears. Let's try them on, but be careful, they're old so they might be a bit delicate.'

Ever so gently, I attached them over Jack's ears. They snapped on easily and when I took my hands away they stayed upright.

'Live long and prosper,' I said to him. He looked at me blankly. 'Before your time, never mind. Now we just need to borrow one of those Robin Hood suits and you'll be good to go.'

Once we'd dressed him up he looked just like any of the Santa's little helpers who swarmed around the workshops building, packing and shipping millions of toys.

'Are you sure this is going to work?' Jack asked anxiously as he attached a small microphone to his vest (we'd 'borrowed' it from an old James Bond Junior Spy Kit).

'Nope,' I said, 'but I don't think you're in any danger, if that's what you're worried about.'

'It isn't. I'm just wondering how long I'm going to have to wear this stupid costume – it itches.' He scratched his back furiously – mostly for effect.

'You'll be fine. Just talk to our suspect as if you're his best friend. Judging by his personal hygiene I suspect no one else will so he'll probably be glad of the company. Don't be too pushy' – which, of course, was like asking water not to be too wet – 'don't bombard him with questions. Just play the "I'm new here too" routine and see if he responds.' I patted him reassuringly on the shoulder. 'Remember, we'll be listening in. If there's any hint of trouble, we'll pull you out of there faster than blackbirds out of a pie, OK?'

Jack nodded once. 'Right, let's do it.'

'Good man. Remember, we're counting on you.'

'So no pressure then.'

'Absolutely not,' I said.

'Good. Now where do I go?'

'You see all those elves over there building toy robots?'

Jack nodded. 'Yep.'

'See the way they're all studiously avoiding that one guy who's attaching the legs?' There was a large elf-free space around our suspect (which didn't seem to bother him in the slightest).

'Yep.'

'Well, he's your guy. Just try not to mention the smell.'

'What smell? Hey, you never told me the guy smelled. How close will I have to get to him?'

'It's not too bad and after a few minutes you won't even notice it. Now get to work.' I pushed him away and into the workshop. Within seconds he'd disappeared into a sea of bright-green elves. I spoke into the microphone that was taped to my jaw. 'Jack, can you hear me OK?'

'Messages are clear; communication will be unbroken this day.' Well at least he was getting into the spirit of things. Maybe he was suited to undercover work; two minutes in and he already sounded like an elf. I just prayed he wouldn't stay like that as I didn't fancy having to listen to elfspeak twenty-four seven; I didn't think my head could take it.

As Jack tried to ingratiate himself with the world's most slovenly elf, I mulled over the case and our progress to date – or, more accurately, our lack of progress. We hadn't really got very far other than establishing that something fishy was going on and the two people closest to Santa were not telling me the entire truth. Santa had clearly been abducted, otherwise why would someone have tried to kill us? But the big questions were why? And indeed who? In terms of the case itself, we still had very little to go on – elf impostor aside. I suspected he was planted purely to keep an eye on things and wasn't a big player in whatever was going on, but he might know something.

There were a few things that we might be able to follow up on though: we'd been attacked by a jet-powered sleigh. It was most definitely a luxury item, so who might have bought one? Surely there couldn't be too many winging their way through the skies – and, after our little adventure, there was probably one less. Mrs C might be able to point me in the direction of flying-sleigh vendors; after all, she had enough of them.

Who dropped the pseudo-elf into the workshop – and why? That one was a long shot, but you never know.

Why were Mrs Claus and Rudolph not telling me the whole story? Although I didn't think they had anything to do with Santa's disappearance, they'd been evasive when I'd asked them about it. They knew something they were unwilling to tell me; but what – and how did it tie into the case?

I sighed in frustration. There was something strange about this case; something I couldn't quite figure out, but I knew I'd get there eventually – as long as I didn't get beaten to a pulp first.

9

Dashing Through the Snow

Wow, electronic surveillance was boring. For an elf-alike, Mr Scruffy was positively taciturn. Not only did he fail to spout the usual meaningless waffle, he barely acknowledged Jack and his replies to the questions put to him were variations on the monosyllabic grunt. If I'd any suspicions that the guy was an impostor, his lack of verbals confirmed it. Through my earpiece, I could hear Jack valiantly – and none too subtly – trying to find out whatever he could without making it too obvious.

'Have you been working here long?'

'Unh-unh.' Which I took to mean no, seeing as he was shaking his head at the same time.

'Where did you work before here? I was in snow globes.' Uh-oh, now he was laying it on with a trowel. Maybe he was getting into character a little too much.

'Unh.' Nope, I have no idea either.

Jack was persisting though. 'No, I mean really. Where did you come from?'

Mr Scruffy evidently found this particular line of questioning a little too direct by elf standards and began to smell an unsavoury rodent of some type. In an instant, he'd pushed Jack away and was running for the door. Seconds later I was after him. Seconds after that Basili was lumbering after me, followed by an indignant Jack. 'Did you see that? He pushed me. I'm not letting him get away with it.'

Privately, I hoped I'd get to him first. An angry Jack Horner was not someone to be trifled with.

Mr Scruffy had raced out of the workshop and across the lobby towards the exit.

'Is he nuts?' I said. 'It's freezing out there.' My question was promptly answered when he grabbed an unsuspecting elf who had just come in and ripped his furs off him. The dazed elf was still standing at the door trying to figure out where his furs had gone as our quarry raced out through the entrance and into the snowy wastes outside.

I skidded to a stop. 'Whoa, let's think about this for a minute, guys.'

'We can't let him get away,' shouted Jack. 'He knows something; I know he does. He might be our only chance.'

Now don't ever say this back to him, but, in this instance, Jack was right. We had little enough to go on – and what little we did have was disappearing into the wilderness outside.

Cold or no cold, we had to follow. I rolled my eyes upwards, nodded to Jack and said, 'OK, let's go get him.'

I pushed the door open and stepped out on to the ice – and promptly slid twenty feet along the ground, legs spinning, like a crazy cartwheel, before landing painfully on my rear. There were hoots of hysterical laughter from behind as my – obviously highly amused – partners took pleasure in my pain. Seconds later I was laughing as well, as they too slid on the slippery surface, tried to grab on to each other for support in a flailing mass of arms and pulled each other down on to the ice – although I did feel a tad sorry for Jack, Basili landed on him.

With as much dignity as I could muster, I carefully stood back up and leaned on a nearby snowdrift for support. As I did so, there was a low humming sound from beyond the drift. I peeped carefully over the edge and almost had my head taken off as a bright red jet ski careened wildly towards me. I barely had time to pull my head back down before it crashed into the edge of the drift above me, covering me in a mini-avalanche of snow, and flew through the air on to the ice beyond. It slid wildly from side to side before the driver eventually recovered control and headed away from me at high velocity.

'He's getting away,' Jack yelled.

I saw my fat fee disappearing in the flurry of slush that was being forced up by the passage of the jet ski – no way; not on

71

my watch; especially not where money was concerned. 'No he's not. We're going to follow him.'

Jack and Basili looked at me as if I was quite mad – which was a distinct possibility.

'What do you suggest we do, run fast? Harry, we'll freeze without proper outdoor gear.' Jack was clearly concerned.

'We'll have to take that chance. We can't afford to let him get away.'

There was a loud roaring from behind us and a familiar voice said, 'Hopefully you won't have to.' Two jet skis pulled up beside us; one piloted by Mrs C, the other by Mary Mary. Slung across the back of both was a heap of furs. The ladies flung the furs at us.

'Get 'em on you, we've no time to waste,' bellowed Mrs C, trying to be heard over the noise of the engines.

I didn't need a second invitation. I quickly donned the furs, threw myself up on the jet ski behind Mrs C and hung on tightly – praying that I wouldn't fall off. Beside me, Basili had joined Mary Mary on hers. A look of disappointment crossed Jack's face.

'What about me?'

Mrs C gave him an affectionate hug. 'Too dangerous, Jack. Your mother would never forgive me if something happened to you. Just keep an eye on things here while we're gone. If we don't make it back, it'll be up to you to break the case. We're counting on you.' It was certainly dramatic, but it had the desired effect. Jack cheered up instantly with his new found sense of responsibility and gave an elaborate salute.

'Yes, ma'am,' he said proudly. 'This case is in safe hands with me.'

Before I could say anything else, there was a sudden jolt as the jet ski lurched forward. I just about managed to stay on by grabbing Mrs C tightly and holding on to her for dear life. If this was what it was like while we were starting, what would it be like when we were racing across the snow? One of those 'This isn't such a good idea' thoughts marched into my mind and demanded my attention. I chose to ignore it, although I knew it was right. If I'd really thought about it, I'd have realised how ridiculous the whole thing was: a city pig like me at the North Pole, risking near death from exposure in pursuit of someone with bad personal hygiene who might (and it was a long shot) just provide a breakthrough in the case, riding across freezing wastes on a jet ski piloted by a woman who claimed to be the wife of a mythical character who brought toys to millions of children once a year. Had I missed anything?

I was bumped, jostled and swung from side to side as we lurched after our quarry. But for the fact that I was gamely trying not to be flung off the violently bucking machine, it didn't feel like we were moving at all. The only things that weren't white were the red dot in the distance that we were just about keeping up with and the four of us. With the furs on, we looked like grizzly bears out for a jaunt on the snow.

Grizzlies on ice! That would make their polar cousins turn their heads and stare in amazement.

'Faster, faster, we're gaining on him,' I roared in Mrs C's ear, hoping she could hear me over the noise of the engine and howling wind. She nodded and gunned the accelerator, trying to squeeze out every last particle of speed we could muster.

Now the jet ski ahead was definitely getting closer. I could make out Mr Scruffy giving an occasional panicked glance behind to see where we were. Not too far was the answer. Only a few more minutes and we'd be right on top of him.

And then what?

How were we going to stop him? He was hardly going to pull over and come quietly. At the speed we were going at, any attempt to force him to stop would probably only end in disaster – more than likely ours. Then I had my brainwave; my gloriously insane, probably-ending-in-certain-death brainwave. I can only claim that the cold had somehow suppressed my cowardice gene and made me temporarily prone to insane acts of bravery.

'Try to get beside him,' I roared at Mrs C. She nodded and gradually drew alongside the red jet ski.

'Keep it as steady as you can,' I shouted as I stood up, blissfully ignorant of the stupidity of what I was about to attempt. I fixed my eyes on Mr Scruffy's jet ski, watching it get closer and closer. Nearly there, I thought. Just a few more seconds.

Now!

I threw myself off our jet ski and made to grab him. As if anticipating my actions – actually, with hindsight, he was definitely anticipating my actions – as soon as I jumped Mr Scruffy hit the accelerator and his craft leaped forward. I sailed through the air and completely missed him. It wasn't a total disaster though, as I did manage to grab on to Basili, whose jet ski had just pulled up parallel to us on the far side. This of course wasn't part of the plan and, since it was entirely unexpected, it caused the jet ski to skew off the ice and up a small slope while Mary Mary vainly tried to wrest it back on course. We crested the top and rocketed into the air while Basili tried to hold on to the back and I tried to hold on to him.

'Mr Harry, what were you thinking?'

'Trust me, Basili,' I roared back. 'It wasn't planned. I was rather hoping to land on the elf's jet ski, not this one.'

'Ah, I am seeing now. Perhaps if I am dropping you, you might be achieving your original aim,' and before I could object he'd grabbed me and flung (*note*: not dropped) me towards the fleeing elf. I closed my eyes and there was a satisfying thump as I made contact with something softish. Seconds later I was lying on the snow gasping for air and thanking whatever gods of fortune had been watching over me that I was still alive, while a muffled voice from somewhere under me shouted, 'Get off, I can't breathe.'

Slowly (I wasn't really too keen to oblige) I rolled off the semi-flattened elf impostor and grabbed him before he could escape again.

'Now wasn't that fun?' I roared in his ear. 'We really must do it again sometime. I do so love winter sports, don't you?'

He snarled in reply. I guess he wasn't as big a fan of snow as I'd thought.

'Now that we're all nice and cosy, I'm going to ask a few questions. If I don't like the answers I get, I'll set my friend on you.' I was quite getting used to the idea of using Basili (as mild-mannered an ex-genie as you're likely to see) as an intimidating threat. What they don't know won't hurt them – especially in this case as Basili wasn't capable of hurting anything. Of course the pseudo-elf didn't know that: the threat was sufficient to transform him into a remarkably talkative subject indeed.

'What's your name?' I asked.

'Porgie,' came the sullen reply. 'Georgie Porgie.'

'Who sent you? Who are you working for?' At last I was finally getting somewhere – or at least that's what I thought. Just as he was answering, there was a loud neighing and snorting noise from above. Something snaked down and grabbed on to Georgie by the chest – a grappling hook. As I watched he was snatched up and away from me. Instinctively, I grabbed his legs and held on tightly. Once again I found myself flying through the air, hanging on to something and grimly willing myself not to lose my grip.

This time, however, my aerial jaunt came to a sudden halt. There was an explosion of white around me as I ploughed into a snowdrift. Unable to maintain my hold, I felt Georgie

Porgie's feet slip through my arms as he was lifted away. Coughing up snow, I managed to extricate myself from the drift just in time to see him get pulled into a sleigh – reindeer-powered this time – which then accelerated away, leaving me to punch the ground in frustration – which hurt as it was a solid sheet of ice with a thin covering of snow.

Ouch!

What was it he'd said as he was pulled away? I tried to make sense of the snatch of speech I'd heard. It sounded like 'ken' or 'king' or 'khan'. At least that's what I thought he'd said. I didn't even know if I'd heard him correctly. It could just as easily have been 'cake' or 'keg'. Either way, it made no sense whatsoever.

As I sat there, freezing and coughing up snow, the other two jet skis arrived – fashionably late. After establishing that nothing other than my pride was hurt, I was bundled on to the seat behind Mrs C and we made our way back to base. I clung on to her solid frame, becoming increasingly despondent. Would I ever get a break in this case?

It seemed like someone up there – other than those who flew around in jet-propelled sleighs – was listening and took pity on me in my hour of need. We had no sooner arrived back at Santa's workshop when Jack rushed out to meet us, waving frantically, clearly excited.

'Harry, Harry,' he gasped, 'it's the Grimmtown police. They called while you were away. They've discovered Santa's sleigh.'

10

CSI: Grimmtown

'**A**s you can see,' said Detective Inspector Jill of Grimmtown PD, 'the sleigh doesn't appear to have crashed. From the impact marks on either side, it does look as if it was forced to land by a person or persons unknown, but they seem to have taken care to ensure that the landing was relatively safe. There is no indication as to what happened to any of the occupants afterwards, but we have found no evidence to suggest that they were injured when the craft went down.'

I could see the relief on Mrs C's face. Now, at least, she had some hope that her husband might still be alive. I walked over to the yellow tape that cordoned off the area around the sleigh and had a good look. It was just as DI Jill had said: the sleigh itself didn't look in too bad a condition, the tracks in the ground behind indicated a clean landing, but of the reindeer or Santa there was no sign. I called DI Jill over.

'Did your forensics guys find anything?'

'C'mon Harry, you know better than that,' she said. 'This is police business. I can't just pass on confidential information to any Tom, Dick or Harry now, can I?'

'Maybe not,' I said, 'but you owe me one. Who gave you the info that let you break the Little Red Hen case? Me. If it hadn't been for me, she'd still be out there.'

DI Jill looked at me for a second, considered her options and rolled her eyes skywards. 'OK, Harry, you win. Forensics haven't found too much. No fingerprints; nothing we might get a DNA sample from; very little trace evidence. Whoever did this went to inordinate lengths to cover up their tracks.'

I immediately picked up 'very little trace evidence'. 'But they did find something?'

Jill said nothing. I could understand that, she could only say so much to me without getting into trouble. On the other hand, the techs might be a different story.

'Mind if I talk to them?' I asked Jill.

She sighed heavily – a do-I-really-have-a-choice kind of a sigh – and lifted the tape to allow me under. 'Why not? They're nearly done, but they were pretty thorough,' she said as I passed by.

'Who's the lead tech?' I asked.

'Crane.'

'As in he of the bright orange head feathers and meaningful silences?' In fact, Crane was so predictably enigmatic that the cops used to play a game when he was working on a crime scene: try to guess which expression he'll use next. The scoring was complicated but could be summarised as: sunglasses on or off = one point, meaningful pause = two points, withering stare = three points, and enigmatic quip = four points. All four at once got a bonus of ten points. The current record stood at thirty-four and I was determined to beat it.

'The same, but you have to admit he knows his stuff,' said Jill.

I didn't doubt it. Grimmtown PD's forensics team was one of the best in the business and Crane was their boss. If they couldn't find evidence at a crime scene then that evidence didn't want to be found. Still, it was worth a shot. Maybe my piggy eyes would pick up on something they'd missed.

'Can I go in now?' I asked.

'Sure, it looks like our guys are packing up so there's no risk of you contaminating the scene.'

I gave Jill an 'as if I would' sort of look.

I walked around the sleigh, examining the ground carefully. The kidnappers had certainly been thorough; all footprints, hoof prints or any other kind of print had been very carefully obliterated. The sleigh itself, dents apart, looked like it had been gone over by a professional valeting service after it had landed. It was sparkling. This meant, in effect, that regardless of how hard I looked, I wasn't going to find anything.

As I examined the sleigh's interior, there was a clearing of a throat from the far side. It was the kind of polite coughing that suggested that the cougher wasn't too pleased to see me, that I was interfering with their work and that they'd much rather I was somewhere else. It had to be Crane.

I looked up into a stern-featured face dominated by a long beak and topped by an unruly mass of bright orange feathers, parted to the right. The eyes were masked by a spanking new pair of sunglasses.

'Dr Crane,' I said, grinning widely just to annoy him further. 'DI Jill said I could take a look around.'

Crane took off his sunglasses and stared meaningfully at me. 'That's Lieutenant Crane.' There was a pause – which I presumed he intended to be more meaningful as he continued to gaze at me. 'What,' another pause, 'are you doing here?' The glasses were put back on. At least now if he continued to stare at me, I wouldn't have to see it – and I was nine points up already.

Small mercies.

'Sorry, Lieutenant, I forgot.' I hadn't, I just did it to annoy him. He was very particular about his title.

'Hmph,' was the indignant response.

'Anyway,' I said, being even more cheerful, 'did you find anything?'

The sunglasses came off again and this time he was giving me a significant stare – which I assumed was one step up the scale from meaningful but still only garnered three points. Now I was up to thirteen and looking good.

'That, my friend,' pause for effect, 'is a good question.' Fifteen.

'I know it is. I'm a detective. It's my job to ask questions, so I'm pretty good at it.'

Another pause and stare (but I couldn't tell if it was withering, significant or another type of stare entirely). Twenty points; record here I come.

'And,' pause, glasses on, 'to answer your question, all we have found so far,' long pause (definitely for effect), glasses off again, 'is tobacco'. Twenty-six; I was on the final stretch, the record was looking good. No, I wasn't enjoying this but I still needed as much information as I could get so, if it meant I had to listen to Lieutenant Crane, then this was a sacrifice I had to make.

'Well, one of my techs found traces of tobacco just behind that rock there.' He waved one of his wings, indicating a large boulder some distance from the sleigh. 'It's ordinary pipe tobacco.' Pause. 'You can get it in any store so it's not much of a lead.' Pause, glasses on. 'It could have been left there by anyone. Once we analyse it in the lab we may know more because that, my friend, is what we do.' Thirty-one points.

'And did your team find anything else?'

I caught a hint of evasion on his face that he quickly masked with his usual blank demeanour. 'No, nothing else.'

There was something, but he wasn't willing to share. I had to find some way of making him change his mind.

'You see that lady over there?' I waved in Mrs C's direction. Crane nodded.

'Well, her husband is the owner of this sleigh and he's missing. Now her style of dress might have given this away already, especially with you being a CSI and all, but the missing man is Santa Claus and, unless we find him in the next twenty-four hours, there are going to be a lot of very disappointed children all over the world. Do you have kids, Dr Crane?'

'Yes,' he replied. 'Three.'

It was time to lay on the guilt trip. 'Do you want to be the one to tell them why they have no presents this year? Why they'll remember this Christmas Day for the rest of their lives for all the wrong reasons? It might even have a traumatic effect on them. Could you live with that? Could you?' I could see I was getting to him. The mention of his kids had made a small crack in his calm exterior and I was about to open it wide. 'This woman has hired me to track down the missing Santa and I'm going to do everything in my power to find him, do you understand?' Dr Crane swallowed once and nodded. 'Good, because every little thing that can help me might take me one step closer to ensuring your kids have a happy Christmas. I know you have to observe standard police protocol here but if you've found something else – no matter how small – it might be the thing that breaks this case.

'Imagine the satisfaction you'll get when we find Santa and you're there helping your kids open their presents, secure in the knowledge that you were the one who gave us that one vital clue.' My patter was working and I could feel he was about to reveal all – in a manner of speaking.

'Well, there was one other thing, but I'm not even sure it's relevant. I won't know for certain until I get it back to the lab.' No meaningful silences and the glasses stayed firmly on his face. Still stuck on thirty-one points: come on, Crane, cut me some slack. 'We found this.' He reached into an evidence bag and pulled something out. He held it out to me for a closer look. 'Please don't touch,' he said. 'You could compromise the evidence.'

I looked at what he was holding in his rubber-gloved wing. 'It looks like a hair,' I said. From what I could see it was a long cream-coloured hair. It looked too thick and rough to be human, and reindeer didn't have hair as long as this so it hadn't come from one of them. Dr Crane ran a feather along the hair. As he did, some particles of fine white dust fell off.

'Any idea what it is?' I asked.

'Not at the moment,' Dr Crane replied. 'It's not human – unless there was a caveman at the crash site. Based on what I know about animal hair – and I am somewhat of an expert – I don't think it's reindeer hair.'

'So what is it and where did it come from?' I mused. 'Maybe it's just coincidence that you found it; after all, it was a national park and I'm sure lots of animals live there.'

'Yes, perhaps, but animals don't have a tendency to use white powder. That doesn't seem like something you'd find in the wild, now does it?'

'True, but what is it? It just doesn't make any sense.' It was reasonable to assume we weren't dealing with something that applied talcum powder after showering; or maybe we were, this case was weird enough as it was without adding cosmetics to the equation. I really needed the results of the hair (and the powder) analysis as quickly as possible. I had a feeling that this – when combined with the tobacco – was the clue that might just break the case wide open. My heart began to thump just a little bit faster and I could feel the sense of anticipation building up inside me. I was near to a breakthrough; I could feel it. Once more, Harry Pigg was on the case.

'Doc, I have one more favour,' I said.

The sunglasses came off once more and I was given a quizzical look. Thirty-five points, we have a winner and a new world record – and without any enigmatic quips either.

'Can you let me know the results of your tests, just this once?' I handed him a business card. 'My number. Call me any time, day or night. I really need this one, and I promise I won't tell anyone about this little conversation, OK?'

The crane looked at me for a long time and finally gave me a brief nod, which I took to mean yes. Then he turned his back on me and stalked over to his team. Clearly the discussion, such as it was, was ended.

Still, I'd gotten something – not a lot, but something – and in this case any lead, no matter how insignificant, was a break. After one last quick look around, I came back over to where the others were waiting.

'Anything, Harry?' asked Jack.

I shook my head. 'Other than a trace of tobacco and a strand of hair the police found, there's nothing else here.' I described the hair to Mrs C and she confirmed that, based on my description, it didn't sound like a reindeer hair. Other than that, no one could offer any suggestions as to what it was. We were going to have to wait until the Crime Lab did their analysis.

Despite the small break we'd just had, I was becoming as frustrated as the Three Bears during a porridge shortage. Every time I thought we were on to something, the lead fizzled out almost as quickly as we got it. Would this case ever get solved? I sank down on a nearby rock and buried my head in my trotters. This wasn't good. My reputation as Grimmtown's foremost detective was at stake but, more importantly, I didn't fancy getting laughed at by Red Riding Hood and allowing her the opportunity to gloat.

After a few minutes of quality self-pity, I turned to the others. 'It doesn't look like we're going to find anything else here.' I could sense their disappointment, I think they'd been hoping for a breakthrough – or at least some solid evidence Santa was still alive. 'Cheer up, folks,' I continued. 'There's no reason to think he came to any harm and whoever brought the sleigh down seems to have gone to a lot of trouble to make sure it got down safely, so there're reasons to be hopeful.' I really wanted to get out of there and back to Grimmtown as quickly as possible and wait for Dr Crane to call me. Reluctantly, they followed me back to our sleigh and, after we were all aboard, we made our way back to the city.

11

A Rug with a View

After we'd landed back at the Claus residence I sent Jack and Basili home in a cab and wandered the streets of Grimmtown, trying to get my thoughts together.

You know those dramatic scenes in movies where the hero is happily minding his own business walking along the street when all of a sudden a really big car screeches up beside him, two burly men jump out, put a bag over his head, bundle him into the car and drive off? Well, I had one of those (sort of). I was walking along the street, minding my own business and mulling over the progress (or lack thereof) in the case. There was a strange swishing noise from above and before I could react, two burly men materialised on either side of me, put a large black bag over my head and bundled me into . . . well, more like on to . . . something soft and wavy. There was a sudden lurch as whatever I was in took off once more and then silence – apart from some whispering.

89

'Is this him?' This was a deep I'm-a-tough-guy-so-don't-screw-with-me kind of whisper.

'How many pigs in trench coats do you see walking around Grimmtown? Of course it is,' whispered a second, just as intimidating voice.

Now I didn't recognise either voice, but I figured they were the types who would do me irreparable damage if I suddenly tried any heroics – not that I was going to try too much while I had a bag on my head.

I could still hear noises from outside the vehicle and could feel the wind buffeting my head, which suggested I was in a convertible of some kind, but I couldn't feel any vibrations or engine noise. It was a very strange sensation. I extended my arms on either side but couldn't feel any doors or walls. Mystified, I ran my trotters across the floor. It seemed to be made of very plush material; possibly a carpet.

Carpet! Of course. I wasn't in the world's quietest sports car after all. I knew exactly where I was and, more to the point, who had abducted me. Yet again I had one of those sinking feelings I knew only too well. Yes, things had gone from bad to very much worse.

'Hi, Ali, can I take the bag off now? I presume we're on your magic carpet.'

There was a brief round of slow, sarcastic applause and then a voice said, 'Of course Harry. My, my, it didn't take you too long to figure out where you were, did it?'

The bag was pulled roughly from my head and I found myself staring straight into the face of one of Grimmtown's biggest gangsters, Ali Baba. Ah yes, now the plot was really thickening. If Ali had me, then my life expectancy was dropping fast to roughly the same level as a haemophiliac's at a vampire convention.

Then, to my complete surprise, Ali said something that I never thought I'd ever hear him say, 'Harry, I need your help.'

'Excuse me,' I said, shock visible on my face. 'Could you repeat that? I'm not sure I heard it properly.'

'You heard. I need your help.' To be fair, he did look as if he was struggling to say the words.

Now this was roughly akin to the fox asking the Gingerbread Man for his assistance, so you can imagine my disbelief. 'Why exactly do you need my help?'

Ali Baba looked at me strangely. 'Presumably you've heard about what happened last night.'

'Not really, I've been out of town,' I said.

He threw a newspaper at me. 'Read the main article.'

I picked up today's edition of the *Grimmtown Gazette* and read the huge headline that dominated the front page.

Crime Wave in the City
Grimmtown Terrorised

That's what I like about the *Gazette* – it doesn't go for sensationalism! I read on.

The citizens of Grimmtown are cowering in fear in their homes today after a spectacular series of robberies across the city last night.

At exactly midnight forty of Grimmtown's wealthiest families and businesses were burgled in a series of elaborate heists. In every case, alarm systems were circumvented and security cameras picked up little or no trace of the intruders. Some blurred and very brief footage that some cameras did record shows what appears to be a single burglar, dressed in a tuxedo entering the premises. Grimmtown PD advise that there isn't enough detail in any of the footage to make an accurate identification. Despite this the police say they are following a definite line of enquiry.

As of now, no precise details of what was stolen are available but the haul is described by a Grimmtown PD spokesperson as 'substantial'.

I looked across at Ali Baba and raised an eyebrow. 'Forty burglaries, forty thieves. It's not much of a stretch, is it? Even Grimmtown PD must have been able to figure it out.'

'Except for one small detail that they appear to have chosen to overlook: I didn't do it.'

I raised my other eyebrow. 'Really?' I have to say, I agreed with Grimmtown's finest here. Even without any evidence, Ali Baba and his forty thieves surely must have been a shoo-in for the crime; the numbers were just too coincidental.

'Yes, really,' Ali Baba continued as we sped through the streets of the city. 'Although I think it's fair to say that even if I and my men had been having dinner with the police commissioner and the mayor last night when these admittedly admirable crimes were committed, they'd probably still have arrested me. Except for the fact that the evidence is, as of now, circumstantial and I have an exceedingly good lawyer, I might still be imprisoned.'

'So what's all this got to do with me?' I asked, although I had a fairly good idea what – and it wasn't something I was particularly looking forward to.

'Quite simply, I think someone is trying to frame me. I want you to find out who actually did these crimes and clear my name.'

'You're kidding, right?'

'Do I look like I'm kidding?'

Actually he didn't – but then again, he never looked like he was kidding. He had that kind of face and he wasn't noted for his sense of humour.

'But I already have a client. I can't abandon her,' I protested, knowing that it was a futile gesture.

'Well, now you have two clients,' Ali replied. 'I can't imagine your caseload is so heavy that you can't manage two clients at once.'

'Well, my current case is proving problematic. I'm not sure I can give you the time that you might reasonably expect in a case of this complexity.'

Ali gave a sigh of frustration and turned to the front of the carpet. 'Sayeed,' he said, 'if you'd be so kind.'

The pilot, who was sitting cross-legged at the front of the craft, nodded once. The magic carpet lurched forward and then began to ascend through the evening sky. In panic I scrabbled around, looking for something to grab on to so as not to plummet down into the streets below. Around me, the two henchmen and Ali Baba seemed totally unaffected by the sudden ascent as they sat on the carpet, laughing at my discomfiture. How come they didn't look scared? And, more importantly, how come they didn't fall off?

Ali must have known what I was thinking. 'Velcro,' he said.

The magic carpet continued to shoot upwards and, as the pilot increased the angle of ascent, I began to slide towards the back of the carpet. Ali Baba showed great courtesy in leaning to one side to allow me to pass him by. I looked up as I zipped past him and caught his eye. He must have taken pity on me as he ordered Sayeed to level out – just before I tumbled off the edge of the carpet. What was it with this case, all these flying vehicles and close shaves?

With an all too familiar sense of resignation – why was I suddenly detective of choice for Grimmtown's crime fraternity? – I nodded to Ali and confirmed that I'd take on the case, although it was not as if I had much of a choice, was it? I either agreed to Ali's terms or became a pork pizza on the street below.

'OK, OK,' I gasped. 'You have my complete and undivided attention. Now, just so we can be clear, you say you weren't responsible for these robberies.' Ali nodded.

'So I assume you have an alibi for midnight last night?'

Ali shifted and looked uncomfortable. 'Well, yes and no.'

'What do you mean "Yes and no"?' I knew it, it had been too good to be true. Here came the wrinkle.

'As I've already said, we weren't responsible for the forty robberies the police are interested in because we were in the process of relieving Danny Emperor's warehouse of his entire stock of gentlemen's clothes. We bypassed the alarms at ten p.m. and spent over four hours cleaning the place out. It was quite a haul.'

'Are you trying to tell me that you didn't commit the forty robberies at midnight because you were busy burgling somewhere else? What kind of an alibi is that?'

'It is a somewhat unfortunate alibi as alibis go, I will admit, but the fact remains, we are not responsible for last night's crime wave, but we can't tell the police why exactly, can we?'

No, I thought, *you were too preoccupied with a smaller one of your own.*

My thoughts were interrupted by the ringing of my phone. With a nod from Ali, I was allowed answer it. 'Hello,' I said. 'Whoever this is, it's not a good time.'

'Harry, it's me: Danny.' Oh well, there was a surprise. I suppose he wanted my help too.

'Danny, can I call you back? I'm in the middle of something here.'

'Please, Harry, just give me five minutes. I've been robbed. It's my warehouse. It's been completely cleaned out.'

'Gee, Danny, that's terrible. Any idea who did it?' Well, I couldn't really say I was looking at the culprit, could I? Not if I didn't fancy going for another flying lesson.

'The cops have no idea, but they don't think it's linked to the other robberies last night.'

'Well, that's good at any rate. Listen I really need to go, can we talk about this later?'

'Harry, please; it's my livelihood. I need your help. Please, tell me you'll take the case.'

Typical: I'd gone from zero to three cases in under a day and I didn't want any of them. Mind you, at least I knew who had robbed Danny – although I wasn't sure I'd be too successful in revealing the culprit. Then I had an idea; it might have been an idiotic idea but it might get me off the hook on at least one of the cases. 'Danny, I'll take your case. Now I really have to go. I'll catch you later, OK?' Before he could say anything else, I hung up.

'Here's the story,' I said to Ali Baba. 'I'll take your case, but my fee is that you return everything you stole from Danny's warehouse.'

Ali's eyes narrowed. 'I think, perhaps, that you may want to reconsider that last statement.'

I reconsidered (for a nanosecond) and ran the options through my head: solve one case immediately – check; give Ali Baba some of my time while I tried to solve his case – check, but then again I didn't have a choice, did I? At least it was an easy way for Ali to get out of paying in the event I did manage to sort out his problem – not that I held out too much hope of solving it; I was more concerned with how to keep Ali sweet while I investigated what seemed like an impossible case – while trying to not run foul of a police force that believed they already had the case wrapped up. Nice!

'No, Ali, I don't think so.' I wasn't sure where this sudden bout of courage had come from, but I'd had just about enough of being pushed around. 'Drop me off the carpet if you want, but my terms are that you return Danny's clothes. Otherwise no deal.' I looked into his eyes wondering if he had the same stare staying power as Rudolph – I hoped not, calling my bluff would put me in a very weak negotiating position (as in being dangled by my ankle from a magic carpet high above Grimmtown).

Ali didn't even try to argue the toss – maybe he felt that me clearing his name was more then recompense for having to part with the spoils of his latest crime. 'Very well, Harry,' he said, with a nonchalant wave, 'it's a deal. Where can we drop you off?'

I sincerely hoped that he was using that phrase as a figure of speech. 'Somewhere near my apartment would be good

– and on the ground,' I managed to croak. A few moments later my feet were firmly on terra firma again. Before I could say anything – a 'thank you' certainly wasn't one of them – the magic carpet was ascending into the darkening sky once more and, for the first time in what seemed like years, I was finally on my own. Wearily, I dragged myself through the front door and up the stairs to my second floor flat. Fumbling the key in the lock, I pushed the door open and fell into the living room, almost literally as I was so exhausted I could barely stand.

12

Sleigh Belles Ring

I'd like to say that that's why I didn't notice there was someone else in the room as any other reason would reflect badly on my detecting abilities, powers of observation and legendary senses that number above the fifth one. In truth, the room was dark, the curtains were closed, I was so relieved to be home I never thought to turn on the light and the intruder was exceptionally quiet. Until a dark voice said, 'Mr Pigg, about time; I've been waiting quite a while for your return,' I'd have probably gone straight to bed without any idea there was anyone other than me in the apartment.

With a kind of resigned how-much-worse-can-this-day-get groan, I turned in the direction of the voice. In the gloom I could dimly make out a shape sitting in my favourite chair. From what I could see, whoever it was was slightly taller than me and was either wearing the biggest turban I'd ever seen or was sporting an afro the size of a hedge. He looked like a giant microphone. Then again, maybe I was just imagining it; I was certainly tired enough. 'Who the hell are you, and why are you sitting in my comfy chair?'

He gave the typical stranger in the apartment reply, 'My name is not important,' and followed it, after a brief pause with, 'and it looked like the most comfortable of your chairs.' He shifted from side to side. 'I suffer terribly from piles.'

'Gee, you have my sympathy; now I'll ask you again, what are you doing here?' I'd had a rough few days, was tired, in need of a shower and looking forward to a good night's sleep; compassion wasn't high on my current priority list – not even for someone with haemorrhoids.

I didn't even care if he had a gun, although I couldn't actually see if he was armed or not. At this stage I just wanted to lie down. In fact, being shot might not be the worst thing that could happen to me just now – at least I wouldn't have to worry about being flung out of vehicles in mid-air any more. I collapsed on to my sofa. I was too far gone to be concerned.

'Close the door on your way out, will you, my good man? And if you intend to search my apartment, can you do it quietly although you won't find anything; I keep all my files in my office.'

'Relax, Mr Pigg. I'm not going to hurt you. In fact, I may be able to help you in your current case.'

'Which one?' I mumbled. 'At the moment, they're piling up like dirty plates in Stiltskin's kitchen.'

'I'm delighted to hear it,' said microphone man. 'But I'm referring to the case of the missing Santa.'

Tiredness rolled off me. Suddenly I was interested. 'What about Santa? What do you know?'

'Patience, patience. All in good time.'

'Look, if you don't mind I could really dispense with the game playing. It's late, I'm tired, you're in my flat uninvited and I don't have time for this nonsense. If you've got something to say, say it now and go.'

'Very well, here's what I have to say – and please forgive the nature of my statement. For reasons that I cannot disclose, it must inevitably be of a somewhat cryptic nature.'

I rolled my eyes, someone else speaking in riddles. Great. 'Go on and then get out.'

'If you need to find Santa then be aware that time is of the essence in this case,' the intruder declaimed.

To be quite honest, I was expecting something a bit less obvious and a bit more helpful. 'Is that it?' I said. 'You broke into my apartment to tell me I needed to get a move on? Tell me something I don't know; something that might actually be of some help. I don't need you to tell me that tomorrow's Christmas Eve; I'm already painfully aware of that, thank you very much.' I wasn't tired any more – apart from tired of this idiot in my living room.

The intruder stood up. 'No you misunderstand; *time* is of the essence here.' This time he emphasised the word 'time'. It didn't really matter, it was still nonsense.

'OK, that's it. You're out of here now. If I need idiotic, pointless statements of the obvious I'll visit a psychic.' I pointed at the door.

'Please, Mr Pigg, I cannot say more. Think about this conversation after you have had some rest. It may make more sense then.' The intruder headed to the door. 'Remember, the future of Christmas is at stake here.'

Really? I hadn't been aware of that either. It was good of him to continue to point these things out, otherwise I might have missed them. I was tired of this. 'Just go.'

'Very well, but consider carefully what I've said.' He walked out and closed the door behind him. He had to turn sideways to fit through.

Time is of the essence, hah! I fell back on the sofa as tiredness made a sneak attack on my recent burst of energy and forced it into an inglorious retreat. Just as I was dropping off, I had the nagging sense that there was something familiar about the intruder's voice – or maybe it was just my imagination. I didn't care any more, I just wanted my bed. Struggling to my feet, I stumbled into the bedroom. At first I was so tired I didn't even notice the low rumbling noise that greeted me when I entered. The aroma in the room, however, jolted me to my senses like a dose of smelling salts had been wafted under my nose.

Had something died in here while I was away, I wondered – and where was that rumbling noise coming from? It sounded like an avalanche was cascading towards me from somewhere. I shook my head to wake myself up and told myself to get a grip. Whatever it was, it was no avalanche.

Through the dim light from the window I could make out a large shape lying on my bed. Further investigation determined that the rumbling noise was emanating from whatever it was. Cautiously I crept towards the bed. As I neared it, the vile smell grew more intense and, accompanying the rumbling noise, I could hear a rhythmic frrppp, frrppp.

All trace of fear evaporated and annoyance took its place. The mysterious noise was the sound of the ex-genie snoring loudly and the other noise was . . . well, I think you can work it out for yourself.

Some thirty minutes later I'd learned something else about my temporary lodger: it was impossible to wake him up when he went to sleep. I'd pulled at him, kicked him, shouted at him, poured cold water on his head, threatened him, pulled all the covers off him and the best I could get from him was a mumbled 'G'way, I'm tired.'

Eventually, frustrated, angry and still very, very tired I went back to my living room and fell into a dreamless slumber on the sofa. Ah bliss; sleep at last – or at least it was until I was awakened almost immediately by a loud banging at my door. This was really turning out to be one of those days – and nights. Now I wasn't even being let have a decent night's sleep.

'Go away,' I muttered, pulling a cushion over my head. It was no use; I could still hear the banging – which seemed to have gotten louder. Whoever it was, they really wanted to see me.

'Call at my office,' I shouted. 'I should be there by nine.' Or probably much later, if I didn't get any sleep.

Strangely, I was too tired to be scared – or maybe it was just that I was all scared out by events over the past twenty-four hours. Either way, the knocking at the door didn't bother me unduly. It could have been an abominable snowman outside and I wouldn't have been too concerned; I just needed my sleep and no one (or nothing) was going to stop me. But the banging continued: **THUMP, THUMP, THUMP**.

Resigned to being awake at least for the foreseeable future, I rolled off the sofa, on to the floor and, eventually, got myself upright.

'I'm coming, I'm coming,' I shouted, trying to be heard over the noise of the knocking. Reaching the door, I went to unlock it and then paused as I decided a bit of caution wouldn't go amiss. 'Who's there? What do you want?' I shouted, hoping I'd be heard over the battering noise that was now threatening to wake up not only everyone in the building but very probably everyone in the neighbourhood too. Although the neighbours were, by now, used to strange things happening in or around my apartment, they still tended to frown upon being woken up in the middle of the night.

'Open up, Harry, it's me.' Over the thumping I could just make out Mrs C's voice.

'Do you know what time it is?' I roared. 'I'd really like to get some sleep.'

'But I've something important to tell you. I've found out who sold that jet-powered sleigh.'

Unlocking the door, I dragged Mrs C inside and pointed her at the sofa. As she sat down she sniffed the air. 'What's that awful smell? And where is that noise coming from?'

'Trust me, you don't want to know,' I said as I sat facing her in my comfortable chair. 'Now, tell me all about the sleigh.'

'Right. I spoke to the guy who makes all our sleighs, Wenceslaus King. He's been supplying us with high-quality vehicles for hundreds of years now. If anyone knows about these things, it's him. I asked him about the jet-powered sleigh and after some huffing and puffing about new-fangled devices and how he wouldn't have anything to do with them (he's a bit of a traditionalist you know), he finally admitted that he knew of one company that manufactures them. Apparently they're new on the market.'

'You don't say. Who would this high-tech sleigh company be?'

'Well, apparently it's called Sleigh Belles and is run by two very successful business women – hence the name.'

'And do we have names for these queens of industry?' I asked.

'Yes, they're called Holly and Ivy, and I've even got an address for them.' She reached into her bag and extracted a folded piece of paper. 'They have a hangar out at Grimmtown Airport and their offices are attached to it.'

'We can go there first thing in the morning. But for now I'm going to try to get some sleep.' I slumped down into my chair and rested my head on a cushion.

'Why don't you go to bed?' Mrs C asked the obvious question, but it would take too long to explain.

'Trust me, this is the best option just now,' I said and closed my eyes once more.

It seemed like only minutes later that a strident ringing woke me up. Was I destined not to get any sleep tonight? To my surprise, when I opened my eyes it was daylight and, instead of Basili's flatulence, I could smell freshly brewed coffee. What was going on? As I tried to wake up and get a grip on the situation a steaming mug was put on the table in front of me and a ringing telephone thrust into my trotter.

Blearily, I put the phone to my ear. 'Hello?'

'Pigg, it's Crane. I have that analysis you were looking for.' I looked at my watch, seven a.m.; wow, he was on the ball early.

'And?' I was still half asleep so my powers of speech were going to be a tad limited for a few more minutes.

'We've done a preliminary investigation and it's definitely not human.' I wondered whether he was taking his glasses off and on while he spoke, but I refrained from asking. 'I'd say it's animal, probably horse but I'll need to do a more detailed analysis to confirm.'

'OK, so we have what could be horsehair, I'm with you so far. Any idea what the white powder is yet?'

'That's more interesting indeed. According to the analysis, the powder is some sort of resin.'

'Resin? As in the stuff gymnasts and weightlifters use for better grip?'

'The very same. Now if you'll excuse me, I need to get this report to the investigating team.' Before I could thank him, he'd hung up. Polite as ever.

I considered what Dr Crane had told me. What did all that mean? The thought of a horse on the parallel bars – even one as graceful as Black Beauty – or doing a clean and jerk with two hundred pounds of weights was so improbable that I dismissed it as highly unlikely in this particular case, although I have to confess I would have paid good money to see it. Resin, horsehair – that combination suggested something but I just couldn't place what exactly it was. It hovered there in my subconscious just out of reach, taunting me. Well, it could wait, another more immediate mystery demanded investigation: who'd handed me the phone and, more importantly, where was the glorious coffee smell coming from?

Master detective that I was, I had the mystery solved in no time, helped in no small way by the fact that Mrs C was in my kitchenette, washing up what I suspected was a week's worth of dirty dishes (I'm very busy, you know, and don't always have enough time for the domestic duties. I'm usually very good around the house).

'Have you been here all night?' I asked her.

'Well, there wasn't much point in going home and then coming back in the morning was there?' Mrs C said. 'Anyway, this place needed a good cleaning. I don't know how you manage to live in squalor like this.'

It wasn't that bad. Sure, there were unwashed dishes in the sink and some underwear drying on the radiators, but I wouldn't have described it as squalor – that was a bit harsh. On the other hand, my apartment was now gleaming. All exposed surfaces had been polished, the floor had been swept and there wasn't any sign of my underwear anywhere. I hoped she'd put it away as opposed to thrown it away.

In fact, the apartment was now cleaner than when I first moved in.

'Um, thanks, but you didn't really have to.'

'Yes, I did; besides it gave me something to do while you and your sidekick snored in stereo. I certainly wasn't going to get much sleep with that racket.'

'I don't snore,' I said indignantly.

'Yes you do, just not as loudly as he does.' She jerked her thumb at the bedroom. 'Honestly, you were like a pair of reindeer. Now get up and drink that coffee, we've work to do.'

I took a sip of my drink – even that was fabulous. It seemed almost a shame to drink it; I wanted to keep it forever and worship it first thing every morning.

'Damn fine coffee.' I raised the mug in tribute.

'It should be: I've had over two hundred years of practice.'

I didn't doubt it.

I tried to drink it slowly, savouring the moment but Mrs C was having none of it. 'Come on, come on, we're wasting time here. We need to get a move on or we'll be late.'

I wanted to say, 'Serves you right for making such good coffee', but it came out as 'Yes, ma'am, just one more sip.' Don't know how that happened!

Minutes later we were in my car and heading for the airport.

'Do you know anything about Sleigh Belles?' I asked.

'Not really, we've never done business with them. We tend to be a bit more traditional. From what I've heard they're very professional and capable. Anything more than that I suppose we'll find out when we get there.'

It didn't take long to reach the airport. After making a few enquiries we were directed to a large hangar on the outskirts of the cargo area. Inside, I could see a handful of jet-powered sleighs undergoing maintenance.

'Looks like the right place,' I said as we headed to a door with a sign which read 'Sleigh Belles – Office. Please ring to enter.'

I rang, the door opened and we entered. Inside the office was warm, comfortable and empty. 'Hello, anyone at home?' I shouted as I walked over to what I assumed was the reception area.

'Just a moment, we'll be with you shortly,' came a voice through a partially open door in the back wall, which I assumed led to the hangar proper. Moments later two dishevelled ladies in oil-stained overalls came in, one carrying a large wrench, the other a welder. As soon as they saw us, they smiled broadly.

'Hi,' said one, a short brown-haired girl extending her hand. 'I'm Holly.'

'And I'm Ivy,' said her tall blonde companion.

'And we're the Sleigh Belles,' they chimed in unison, dazzling us both with gleaming smiles.

'Whether it's a commercial cargo sleigh,' said Holly.

'Or a small, private sleigh,' said Ivy.

'Then Sleigh Belles have just the sleigh for you,' again in unison. 'When it comes to choosing a sleigh, the Belles will show you the way.'

I didn't know about anyone else, but I was threatening to overdose on the saccharine diatribe of the Sleigh Belle girls. As I listened to them I could feel my blood-sugar level rising. I wondered who their PR people were so I could find them and beat them to a pulp for coming up with that jingle. It was the least I could do.

'OK, ladies, enough with the sales pitch; we're not here to buy.'

Their faces dropped but only for a moment. Within seconds their innate (and annoying) perkiness was once more to the fore.

'Well, how else can we help? That's what we're here for,' twittered Holly.

'We're interested in your sleighs, or rather in who's been buying them,' I said.

Ivy's face dropped and she shook her head. 'Oh no, I'm afraid we couldn't possibly give you that information, it's confidential.'

I tried the guilt trip once more. After I'd delivered yet another passionate speech about how Christmas would be ruined for all the children of the world and the poor woman beside me was suffering because her husband was missing (I was quite good at it by now), I was greeted by more firm shakes of the head from both girls and another definitive 'no'. Wow, they were a tough audience.

It was time for Plan B. I turned to Mrs C. 'Perhaps your powers of persuasion might be a tad more effective.'

Within seconds both Holly and Ivy were resting their chins on Mrs C's forearms while she pinned them against the wall, their legs kicking frantically. Well, I'd found it an effective means of persuasion so I was sure Holly and Ivy would too. And as things turned out I was right. Within a few seconds of Mrs C doing her stuff, we were going through

Sleigh Belles records – or should that be record, as they'd only sold one jet-powered sleigh since opening for business.

'It's a very exclusive market, you know,' trilled Ivy by way of excuse. 'Not many people can afford one.'

'You don't say.' I reached for the Sleigh Belles ledger and scanned the first page. It didn't take long as the number of entries could be counted on the fingers of one finger. The only sale they'd made was to a company with a suitably generic and meaningless name, Sleigh Aviation. From the sound of it, I was sure the name was a fake and a quick call to Sol Grundy confirmed my suspicions. Sleigh Aviation didn't exist. I hadn't expected anything else, but I asked him to dig a bit deeper to see what he could find out about them. After thanking him, I hung up and updated Mrs C on what he'd found (or hadn't found if I was to be accurate). Her disappointment was plain.

'All is not yet lost, Mrs C.' I turned to Holly and Ivy. 'If someone was looking to repair one of your sleighs, where would they go?'

'Oh, it depends on the damage,' Holly said. 'What kind of repairs are you talking about?'

'A jet engine clogged up with dozens of . . . what were they called again, Manolos?'

Mrs C nodded a mournful confirmation as she recalled her shoes' fate.

The Sleigh Belles didn't bat a fake eyelash. 'Goodness, then they'd almost certainly have to come to us. We're the only ones that could do that kind of repair. It's very specialised, you know.'

I didn't doubt it. 'If anyone makes enquiries about fixing a jet engine then you're to give me a call right away,' I said. 'Otherwise you know what will happen?' I nodded in Mrs C's direction. 'And we wouldn't want a repeat of that now, would we?'

'No,' chimed both girls, clearly unimpressed at the prospect.

'Good, I'll be waiting for your call. Bye now.' I turned and headed for the door, Mrs C close behind.

For some reason the girls seemed relieved that we were leaving. Now why ever could that be, I wondered?

13

A Run Across the Rooftops

On our way back into town I filled Mrs C in on Dr Crane's call. She was just as confused as I was. 'Horsehair and resin? That's a strange combination.'

Again, the sense of familiarity taunted me but when I tried to focus on it, it slithered away once more. I knew that it should mean something, but what just wouldn't come to me. I'd have a look on the Internet when I got to the office and see if that would suggest anything. As I drove, I told Mrs C about my mysterious nocturnal visitor.

'He said "Time is of the essence." Any idea what that means?' I asked her.

She shook her head, but yet again I got the feeling she was holding something back. What was it with this case and people being evasive? I was used to criminals not telling the truth, but when it was your client or those supposedly helping you . . . Still, I couldn't really accuse her on the basis of my feeling, could I?

I caught a glimpse of something in my rear-view mirror that vanished almost as quickly. Was I being followed? I couldn't see any sinister types in any of the cars behind, nor did any of the vehicles give the impression they were tailing me. Just as I relaxed, thinking I'd imagined whatever it was, it happened again. This time I got a better look: it wasn't a car, it was a carpet. I was being tailed from above.

Ali Baba! I'd forgotten about him – and he wasn't someone you could easily forget. If I didn't show him I was doing something, I could well be falling from that selfsame carpet sometime later in the day. In desperation, I reached for the phone once more. It was a long shot but maybe Detective Inspector Jill might have some info that hadn't been released to the press; something I might be able to use.

'Hey, Jill, it's me, Harry.'

'Harry Pigg, twice in two days. This is quite an honour.'

'Look, Jill, I need another favour, I'm in a bit of a bind.'

I could almost hear her eyes roll upwards. 'What is it now?'

'I've taken on another client since we last spoke and he's very interested in me solving his particular dilemma as soon as possible.'

'Well, let me be the first to congratulate you.' Jill's voice dripped sarcasm – and I can spot sarcasm at a hundred paces. 'But how does that involve me?'

'Because you suspect him of forty robberies; crimes, I might add, he claims he's innocent of.'

There was a sharp (and, I think, impressed) intake of breath. 'Ali Baba, wow, as clients go that one's a doozy.'

That's not how I would have described him but I wasn't in a position to discuss semantics with Jill. 'Look, he says he didn't do it and he wants me to prove it. I have evidence to show that he is innocent but I'm not in a position to share it just at the moment.' Primarily because the evidence suggested he was busy committing another crime altogether – but I wasn't going to tell her that. 'I just need you to give me something to work with, anything. Please.'

The silence from the other end of the phone suggested that not only did Jill have something, but she was considering whether or not to share it with me. I tried to help her make up her mind. 'Please, Jill. If he's innocent then I need to help him. I know he's a crook, but just not on this particular occasion.' Just ask Danny Emperor!

'OK, Harry, but bear in mind that I'm putting my ass on the line here. Make sure it doesn't get back that your source was me.'

'My snout is sealed.'

'All right. Here's the weird thing about this case: CCTV footage didn't capture too much, but what it did capture seemed to suggest that the thieves were identical to each other, all dressed in tuxedos.'

I was confused. 'You mean they looked similar?'

'No, I mean identical; same height, same clothes, same shoes, same everything. It was like the robberies were committed by clones or something – but that's ridiculous.'

I had to agree with her. Whoever had committed the crime, it probably wasn't the result of a bizarre scientific experiment. 'Just so as I'm clear, you're saying that the perpetrators were exactly the same in every respect.'

'Yep, but bear in mind we only caught glimpses of the thieves on camera but what we did see suggested they were.' Now I was even more confused, but I could also see why the police liked Ali Baba for the crimes. Forty apparently identical thieves committing burglaries at exactly the same time at forty different locations: how bizarre was that? Then again it couldn't be any more bizarre than a missing Santa, a reindeer with an attitude problem and jet-powered sleighs, could it?

I thanked Jill and hung up. Where did I go from here? Neither case seemed to be on the verge of a breakthrough and both had anxious clients – although they were anxious in very different ways, it had to be said. As I mulled things over, I caught a glimpse of a huge advertising hoarding on the side of the road. It was an ad for Olé 'King' Kohl and his Fiddlers Three. They were giving a Christmas recital at the Grimmtown Cauldron later today. The hoarding showed Olé and his boys mugging for the camera and waving their violins around. My brain began to make connections. Musicians; horsehair and resin, critical components in violin

118

bows; did I finally have a useful clue? Once more I reached for the phone. It rang twice and was followed by a 'yes' and a meaningful pause.

'Lieutenant Crane, it's Harry Pigg again.' This time I wasn't counting.

'Yes, Mr Pigg, and what can I do for you now.'

'Your horsehair and resin, I think they come from a violin bow.'

The pause this time was definitely sarcastic (remember, I can sense it).

'Violin bow? Mr Pigg, that,' pause, 'is something we're already aware of.'

'Already aware of? Well, why didn't you tell me.'

'Because, my friend, you're a detective. What kind of scientist would I be if I didn't allow you to do some detecting – and you appear to have done a fine job. It took you less than a day to discover something I knew at the crash site. My congratulations.'

I didn't give him time for any more meaningful or sarcastic pauses, I just cut him off. Smartass.

If I wasn't confused before, I certainly was now. Had Santa been kidnapped by a mad, jet-sleigh-flying, Christmas-hating musician? If so – and it did sound unlikely – then why? And more to the point, how was I going to get him back? On top of that I had to find forty identical, monkey-suit-wearing cat burglars or be at the receiving end of Ali Baba's displeasure. Some days it's just great being me.

As if someone up there was reading my mind and felt I needed some more incentive, my phone rang once more. When I answered it, I couldn't hear anything. Great, one of those calls. 'Hello, whoever you are, I'm not that kind of pig.' I expected to hear heavy breathing but instead I got what sounded like someone whispering.

'Mr Pigg, is that you?'

'Yes, who is this? Speak up, I can't hear you.'

'It's me, Ivy from Sleigh Belles, and I can't talk because . . . well, remember you asked us to phone you if anyone enquired about getting their sleigh repaired?'

I was all businesslike now. 'Yes, are they there now?'

'Yes, that's why I'm whispering; I don't want him to hear me. Holly is trying to keep him occupied for as long as possible. Can you get here as quickly as you can?'

'I'm on my way.' I turned the car and did a very unsubtle and highly illegal U-turn in the middle of the freeway and headed back towards the airport.

As I accelerated, Mrs C grabbed the door and held on tightly. 'What's going on?' she demanded.

I quickly filled her in as we raced in and out through the traffic, flirting with several traffic offences but not committing to any. We made it back to the airport in half the time and I parked the car where it couldn't be seen by anyone in Sleigh Belles. As I got out, I turned to Mrs C. 'Stay here, things might get a bit hairy.'

She snorted indignantly. 'No chance. If there's any possibility that this might lead us to my husband, then I'm going with you.' She flexed her arms, which I took as both a threat and signal of her intent. I also knew when I was beaten so I nodded and told her to stay close. 'And under no circumstances are you to go wandering off on your own, regardless of what happens.' I wasn't too concerned for her safety, I wanted to make sure that we were able to keep whoever was in Sleigh Belles conscious long enough to get information out of them. If Mrs C got her hands on them, there was a distinct possibility they wouldn't last the day.

We skirted round a large warehouse and ran towards the Sleigh Belles main entrance, crouching low to avoid detection. When we got to the door, I stuck my head up and peered through the window. A very nervous Ivy was behind the counter casting anxious glances back into the maintenance area. I tapped on the glass gently and when she saw me she waved me inside. I opened the door a fraction and sneaked in, followed by Mrs C.

'Who's in the maintenance hangar?' I whispered.

'Holly and one of the guys who originally bought the sleigh. He wants the engine fixed and she's trying to keep him talking.'

'OK, you stay here while I take a look.' I crept to the door that separated the office from the hangar and peeped through. At first I couldn't see anything other than sleighs, bits of sleighs, sleigh engines and tools for fixing sleighs.

Then I heard voices from behind a large sleigh to my left. If I wasn't mistaken (and I rarely am), it was the same craft that had indulged in the aerial acrobatics with us two nights ago. The dents certainly suggested so. Making sure I didn't step on anything that might give my presence away, I slunk up against the fuselage and inched my way forward.

Now I could make out the voices. One was clearly a nervous Holly, trying her best to stall and doing a very bad job of it. The other was a man's voice and, by the sound of it, becoming increasingly frustrated by Sleigh Belles' actions.

'Can't you be more specific?' demanded the male voice. 'To me it seems obvious: one of the engines is faulty. We collided with a flock of birds and we need to get it looked at.'

'Flock of birds,' a likely story.

'Well, um, it's not as simple as that,' stammered Holly. 'We don't have the parts here. I'll have to order them and that will take . . . um . . . a few days.'

'What do you mean, you don't have the parts? Surely, parts for a jet engine are standard operating procedure? You sell jet-powered sleighs, don't you?'

'Yes but the flange inductor has been totally wrecked and the hyperfilters look like they have what appears to be the heel of a very expensive boot embedded in them. These aren't the kind of things that happen to engines every day, you know.'

Well, that was true anyway.

'Flange inductor? Hyperfilters? There are no such things. You're making this up.' He did have a point, from where I stood it sounded like Holly was reaching a bit. It was time to do something and fast, otherwise the girl was in big trouble.

Just as I was about to finally get a glimpse of the sleigh owner there was a loud clanging noise from behind me, followed by a sheepish 'sorry'. I knew I hadn't made the noise because I was being very careful – and as a detective I was a master at sneaking around – so the noise could only mean one thing.

I looked around at Mrs C. 'I thought I told you to stay in the office,' I whispered.

'You did, but I had to see what was happening out here.' Mrs C was trying to be indignant but she knew she'd fouled up. 'Sorry,' she said once more.

'Well, you're about to get your wish,' I said as the owner of the voice raced around the sleigh to see what had made the noise. 'Who the hell are you?' demanded a very tall man in a very dapper tuxedo. 'And why are you spying on me?' Tuxedos? What was it with tuxedos and my cases? Now, however, wasn't the time to contemplate the ins and outs of sartorial elegance as a large, tuxedoed man was heading straight for me, arms outstretched – and I didn't think he was asking me to dance.

I'd like to say that my next move was planned and superbly executed, but as my attacker lunged at me I slipped on the selfsame pipe Mrs C had knocked to the ground seconds before. The pipe shot backwards and I shot forwards, slipping under the clutches of Mr Tuxedo and colliding with his stomach. There was a satisfying explosion of breath and he fell backwards on to the ground. Before I could grab him – or at least fall on top of him – he rolled to one side and pushed himself upright once more. I swung an arm at him but he easily avoided it. Rather than risk further entanglements, he turned on his heels and sprinted for the hangar entrance.

'Stop that man,' I shouted, but as the only other three people in the hangar were watching him go from a very safe distance, it was a pointless request.

As I stood trying to figure out why he looked so familiar, I received a nudge – no, a jab – in the side. 'Well, what are you waiting for?' said Mrs C. 'Get after him.'

Rolling my eyes upwards in that world-famous gesture of resignation, I lumbered after my retreating quarry, hoping that the burst of speed he was displaying was just an adrenalin rush and he'd soon slow down.

How wrong was I? He must have been a marathon runner in his spare time as he seemed to go faster. There was no chance of me catching him but I figured I'd better make the effort or face the wrath of Mrs C again – not something I was too keen on. I struggled pigfully after him as he ran around sleigh machinery towards the open doors. If he got outside I'd never catch him, so I figured I'd better come up with something fast. Maybe if I could slow him down somehow

. . . ah, the old throw something and knock him out trick. That might work. I grabbed a hammer off a table as I ran – well, jogged – past and, pausing to take careful aim, I flung it at the escaping well-dressed gent. It completely missed him and I groaned in exasperation.

But I was too quick with my frustration. The hammer sailed past him but then rebounded off the frame of a stripped-down sleigh, spun up into the air, deflected off the overhead light and plonked down on his head. Did it stop him? Of course not; I'd never be that lucky, but it did slow him down. I suspect having a hammer bounce off your skull will do that. The success (sort of) of my devious plan fuelled me with a fresh burst of energy and I raced after my staggering prey once more, hoping to nab him before he recovered.

Behind me, Mrs C was roaring, 'Go on, Harry, you nearly have him.' It was an exaggeration of sorts and I was also aware that she wasn't doing too much to help by way of joining in the chase either; I was still on my own. Typical.

I ploughed on, weaving through maintenance tables and bits of sleigh, hoping against hope that I could catch this guy. I really needed a break in the case and this was the only one that I was likely to get between now and a deadline I had no control over – Christmas Eve would fall on Christmas Eve regardless of what I did and it needed a Santa if it was going to work properly.

And the only link I had to getting Santa back was haring out of the hangar. If I didn't catch him Christmas was a bust.

I reached the hangar doors seconds after Mr Tuxedo. Racing out into the cold winter air I looked around but couldn't see any sign of him. Stretching away on both sides of me were other hangars, none close enough to have been reached before I got out. In front of me a short taxiing route led to the main airport runway. He wasn't running down that either, so where the hell was he? I was pretty sure he hadn't vanished into thin air – although that was always a possibility in my cases – so he had to be here somewhere. I looked around again, more carefully this time. Hangars, runway and no obvious place to hide. Or maybe I was wrong. A heap of wooden crates was stacked between Sleigh Belles' hangar and the one to the left of it. It was the kind of thing that a man on the run might use as cover.

'I have you now,' I whispered, as I approached the crates.

If he wasn't there I'd be gobsmacked, so I was gobsmacked when I threw myself around the boxes and leaped on to . . . well, nothing actually. There wasn't a sign of him. There was, however, a ladder leading to the hangar roof and when I looked up I caught a glimpse of his heels as they disappeared from view above me. This was just so unfair: now I had to climb as well. I grabbed a rung and began to ascend. About halfway up I had a horrible thought, what if he's waiting at the top for me to stick my head up? I'd be a sitting pig. Then I'd be a falling pig, followed by a pizza pig on the asphalt below. Before I could think about it I was interrupted by a shout from below.

'He's running along the roof. If you don't get your finger out he'll escape.' Mrs C. was watching out for me once more.

Well at least I knew I wasn't going to be ambushed.

I clambered up the remaining rungs as fast as I could and scrambled on to the roof – just in time to see the well-dressed man leap on to the next hangar beyond and continue running. No matter how optimistic I was, I knew I had no chance of catching him this way.

'Bring the car around and try to get to the last hangar before him,' I roared at my fan club below. 'We might be able to head him off before he gets back to ground.'

Seconds later, as I ran across the roof, I heard a screech of tyre rubber as Mrs C accelerated around the hangar and shadowed me from the ground. I waved her on, urging her to speed up and not follow me, but she just waved back, grinning broadly. It's possible she may have misunderstood my intentions. 'Go faster,' I roared at her. 'Don't wait for me otherwise he'll get away.'

I could see the 'Oh, right' expression as the penny finally teetered on the edge for a few seconds before falling into the vast chasm of her mind. Almost immediately, she gunned the accelerator and the car sped forward, racing parallel to the hangars.

Mr Tuxedo reached the edge of the roof. Did he stop and turn around with his hands in the air, acknowledging that he had no way of escaping and that I finally had him? Did he hell. He didn't even break stride as he jumped across the gap and on to the next building.

I followed and, as the gap didn't look too wide, I leaped without fully contemplating the consequences. I barely made it across to the adjoining roof, teetering on the edge, arms flailing before I managed to regain my balance.

And so we continued our not-so-merry chase across the maintenance hangars of Grimmtown Airport. He managed the gaps with a degree of flair and athleticism; I managed them by gritting my teeth, closing my eyes and jumping – all the while hoping for the best.

Now my quarry had run out of hangars to run across. He'd reached the edge of the last one and, unless he had a well-concealed jetpack under his jacket, the only way was down. Mr Tuxedo took a quick look over his shoulder to see where I was and didn't even slow down before throwing himself off the edge and disappearing from view. I ran to where he'd jumped, fully expecting to see him soar gracefully into the sky, give me a rude gesture and disappear over the horizon. I was wrong on all three counts. When I looked down I saw that his jump had taken him into the back of a truck filled with packing crates. How lucky can you get!

He didn't even waste time checking for injuries. No sooner had he landed than he was up and out of the truck and racing across the asphalt. At the same time, Mrs C roared around the corner, her eyes firmly fixed on the road ahead.

Well, if he could do it . . . I took a deep breath, tried not to think about what I was about to attempt and threw myself off the roof. As I fell, the truck driver took it upon himself to drive away and I watched in horror as my nice soft landing suddenly became something altogether more concrete.

I screamed, closed my eyes, covered my head with my trotters and prepared for the impact I didn't even think I'd feel. To my surprise and relief, instead of splattering across the ground I bounced off something and was catapulted into the air once again. I opened my eyes once more and looked down at the soft-top roof of my car which Mrs C had driven right into my path and I had oh-so-conveniently landed on. At first I was mentally congratulating her on her ingenuity and lateral thinking in coming up with such a stunning rescue plan but quickly scrubbed that train of thought when, oblivious to both my presence and her part in my rescue, she kept driving. With a horrible sense of déjà vu I spun in the air and dropped towards the ground again – luckily from not quite the same height as my first descent. This time my fall was broken by the asphalt, but at least, when I finally managed to sit up and check for injuries, it seemed like that was all that had been broken.

There was a screaming of brakes from up ahead, followed almost immediately by the sound of a car reversing. Seconds later Mrs C pulled up beside me. 'How did you get down so fast?'

I didn't bother to fill her in; I dived into the passenger seat and roared at her to drive. The car sprang forward and we raced along the asphalt, trying to spot where our quarry had got to.

'I can't see him any more,' said Mrs C. 'I think we've lost him.'

I scanned the area ahead of us and caught a glimpse of our quarry nimbly scaling a wire fence on the far side of the runway and disappearing into a maze of buildings beyond. I punched the dashboard in frustration. 'Dammit.'

Mrs C put a sympathetic arm around my shoulders. 'Don't worry about it; we're getting closer to breaking this case all the time.'

'Really? The only thing we were close to breaking this time was my spine when I bounced off the car – and he still got away, whoever he was.' As I said it, the feeling that I'd seen him somewhere very recently sat in the shadows of my mind and taunted me.

'You'll catch him, I know you will.'

I appreciated her support but didn't share her confidence. 'Come on, let's get out of here.'

I sulked all the way back into town. In fact I was seething so much I almost missed it as we drove by.

'Stop, stop the car!' I ordered.

'We're on the freeway, Harry. I can't stop.'

'Well, pull in; do something. Just stop the car.'

'Why? Are you not feeling well?'

'Pull over now.'

Mrs C drove on to the hard shoulder and stopped the car. 'What's going on, Harry? You're behaving very strangely.'

I pointed up at the huge hoarding we'd stopped under; the same hoarding I'd noticed on the way out earlier. 'It's him, look. Up there.'

'It's who? Where? What are you talking about?'

I grabbed her head and pointed it at the huge poster of Olé 'King' Kohl and His Fiddlers Three. 'There? See the grinning idiot second from the left? The guy that looks like his family tree has no forks? That's him; that's the guy we were following at the airport. He's part of Kohl's band.'

'Are you sure about this?' Mrs C didn't seem to share my conviction.

'Positive. It's him all right. Let's get back to town. I need to find out as much as I can about these guys. I'm not sure how they fit into all this but I'm going to find out.'

14

Another Chapter in Which Nothing Unpleasant Happens to Harry

Stiltskin's Diner was the kind of place that gave good food a bad name and then got sued for slander. That was why I only ever drank the coffee there, but it was really good coffee. Mug clenched in trotter I slid into his usual booth and stared at Boy Blue, failed shepherd, dodgy musician and officially the world's worst informant. At least today he acknowledged me – if you consider a grunt to be a sign of recognition.

'Blue, you're looking good this morning.' It was a lie; he never looked good but I had to start somewhere.

Another grunt.

'Have you come across Olé "King" Kohl in your travels around the Grimmtown music circuit?'

'Kohl? Met 'im once or twice. Arrogant. Plays jazz.'

'Isn't everyone who plays jazz arrogant? Seeing as it sounds like musical vomiting I think they try to appear superior so they don't have to explain it.'

Blue nodded. 'Maybe, maybe.'

'So what do you know about Kohl?'

'Used to be known as Oliver Cole back in the day. Small-time thief who 'ad ambitions to be something bigger until he got caught. Spent some time in prison and when he came out changed his name to Olé Kohl, formed that band with his fiddling buddies and went on the circuit.'

'That's it?'

'That's it.'

'Turned away from a life of crime?'

'I didn't say that, did I?'

'Well, what are you saying?'

'All I'm sayin' is that if you checked for burglaries in the towns he's been tourin' you might just see a connection.'

So Cole/Kohl was still keeping his hand in – and his group wore tuxedos. I couldn't see a direct correlation, but I thought I'd ask anyway. 'Any chance he could be involved in that spate of robberies around town the other night?'

Blue looked at me. 'Possible, yes, but it's a bit out of his league unless he had some serious connections – and I don't think he's that well connected.'

Maybe, maybe not, but it was certainly worth following up. 'OK, Blue, thanks for your time.'

I drove back to the office and met up with Mrs C, Basili and Jack.

'Here's where we're at – or not at might be more accurate,' I said to them. 'Santa was kidnapped and the only lead we had was the jet-powered sleigh that attacked us on the way to the North Pole.'

Nods all around.

'Following up on the sleigh lead has brought us to Olé "King" Kohl and his band of merry men who, based on their track record, I like better for Ali Baba's robberies even if I still can't see how they did it or if they're actually involved at all.' I pushed myself away from the table and stood up. 'It's all so confusing. My senses say the two cases are connected in some way, I just can't see how or why.' More – slightly more confused – nods and Mrs C shifted uncomfortably in her chair. Was it my imagination or did she look just a little bit guilty? Again I had the feeling she knew more than she was telling and now, in front of the others, wasn't the time to confront her – but very soon it would be. I was hitting a solid wall in this investigation and I was getting fed up with being blocked every time I thought I had a break.

I also had Ali Baba to consider. He'd already been on the phone once today, demanding progress and issuing his usual brand of exotic threats. I knew he was keeping a close eye on me too and I needed something for him as well or face another exciting magic carpet ride.

'So where do we go from here?' asked Jack.

'Good question,' I said. 'I think a trip to Mr Kohl and his boys is in order. They might let something slip.'

'But they might know you're on to them. It could be dangerous.'

I was tempted to respond with 'Danger is my middle name,' but I refused to resort to cliché at a time like this.

Well, nothing ventured nothing gained. 'It's the only option we have at the moment. Anyway,' I said with as much confidence as I could muster, 'I can take care of myself.'

From the sceptical glances I got, I could tell they remembered the sleigh incident, the jet ski and the recent pursuit at Grimmtown Airport shambles and, perhaps, weren't as convinced as I was.

Unbelievers!

I rubbed my trotters together. 'Right, let's get cracking.'

Mrs C stood up. 'It's about time,' she said.

'Well, I'm sorry things aren't moving as fast as you'd like,' I snapped, indignation rising.

'No, you don't understand; it's really about time,' and she gave me a significant look.

Was she trying to tell me something?

About time? Time is of the essence here? What was it with these people and their insistence that time was so important?

Suddenly, synapses that had previously been on an extended holiday began to arrive back at work.

Time is of the essence here.

It's about time. No, what she meant was, it's about Time.

How could one man single-handedly deliver presents to every child in the world over the course of a single night? Time.

How could one (or perhaps four) men dressed in tuxedos carry out robberies in forty different places at the same time? Time, that's how.

It was indeed all about Time – or, more accurately, the ability to manipulate time.

Satisfied that their work was done, the synapses in my brain headed off for a well-deserved rest.

I turned to Mrs C. 'It is about Time after all, isn't it? Your husband can do something with time and that's how he does what he does. More to the point, that's probably why he was kidnapped. Kohl and his boys are using that same ability to pull off all those robberies and frame Ali Baba at the same time.'

Mrs C nodded and gave me a half-smile. 'I'm sorry I couldn't tell you about it. Each generation of Santas is born with the ability to freeze time. It's been kept a secret for thousands of years and the family have sworn a blood oath never to reveal it to outsiders – whatever the cost. If the secret was revealed, there could be terrible consequences. Think what someone could do if they found out.'

I think I knew exactly what would happen – actually, had happened – if someone found out.

'Rudolph and I probably bent the rules a little by dropping those cryptic hints, but we can safely say that we didn't tell you outright. That way we adhere to the spirit of our vow, but I can't tell you how much it hurt me not to be able to reveal the secret – even at the expense of my husband's life.'

Tears began to trickle down her face; tears that could at any second become a raging torrent.

I seized the box of tissues once more and thrust it at Mrs C. She grabbed a bunch and dabbed her eyes. I tried to reassure her, if only to try to stop the impending deluge. Then I homed in on something she'd said.

Rudolph and I? When had that arrogant herbivore ever tried to help me? Then it hit me: he'd been my mysterious midnight caller – the human microphone. It hadn't been a turban or an afro; it had been a poor attempt to disguise himself by covering his antlers. At least now things were beginning to make a bit more sense.

'Look, we've had a few big breaks this morning,' I said, trying to console Mrs C. 'All we need to do now is confront Kohl like we planned, and hopefully we'll be able to wrap everything up by this evening.' I wished I was as confident as I was making out, but it seemed like the only course of action open to us.

'I hope so,' she sobbed. 'If my husband's not in the air by midnight, there won't be a Christmas.'

I looked at her in horror; I'd forgotten it was Christmas Eve. We didn't have much time left. There's always something.

'We'd better get a move on then,' I said, trying to sound confident. 'Next stop "King" Kohl's. Everyone ready?'

More noncommittal grunts, nervous nods and general I-don't-think-this-is-such-a-good-idea type facial expressions.

'OK then, let's go.'

Jack Horner raised a tentative hand. 'Um, aren't you forgetting something?'

'What's that, Jack?'

'Well, we're about to go after a bunch of thieves and track them to their lair, right?'

I nodded. 'More or less, yes.'

'Well, I don't want to sound like a scaredy cat, but they're probably big tough guys and we're, well, we're not.'

'Now, Jack, did you honestly think that I was going to face these guys unprepared?' In fact, until he mentioned it, I was, but I wasn't going to let my veneer of invincibility get tarnished so easily in front of my team. I wasn't sure exactly how dangerous facing Kohl would be but it probably made good sense to have some degree of insurance before going in there. But who could I call on on such short notice? My usual able assistants in situations like this, Mr Lewis and Mr Carroll, had told me they'd be unavailable until after Christmas.

Aha!

I called Jack over. 'I have a little job for you; here's what I want you to do.' I bent down and whispered in his ear.

His eyes widened. 'You sure he'll be OK with it?'

'Yep, especially when you tell him why we're doing it. Don't worry, you'll be fine.'

Jack scurried out of the door. 'Where's he off to?' asked Mrs C.

'Plan B,' I said.

'Ah, so you actually have a Plan A then?'

'I always have a plan,' I replied, although I could have added: *the plan may be flimsy, improvised, not fully thought out at the time and subject to change depending on events*. It might not have been the most inspiring thing to say, especially right now.

'While Jack's busy, you guys are with me. Basili, when we get there, act the tough guy once more.'

Basili looked unhappy. 'Where is this there that we are going to, Mr Harry? And why must I be acting the gentleman of toughness once more?' This was followed by an extended and unpleasant bout of flatulence.

'We are going to the Grimmtown Cauldron and you are pretending to be the tough guy because you did such a fine job at the North Pole,' I said, and because I don't have time to get anyone else at such short notice – but I left that part unspoken; his ego was fragile enough as it was.

'Right, everyone, now that that's been sorted, let's get to the car and start making tracks.'

15

A Night at the Jazz

We left the office, tramped down the stairs (somewhat reluctantly, it has to be said) and got into the car. As we drove to the Cauldron, I could sense the unease in the other two. It was hard to blame them; I wasn't really sure what I was going to do myself. I didn't really expect them to have Santa trussed up in the front row of the auditorium, but if the guy we'd chased at the airport saw me he might panic and do something stupid. Then again, he might just beat the living daylights out of me – and I didn't think my 'minder' would do much by way of minding. I suspect his concept of minding in that instance would be running for the door as fast as he could. Ho hum.

The Cauldron itself was an auditorium that looked like a giant cauldron turned on its side. It stood on a hill overlooking the city and was the venue *du jour* for Grimmtown's musical set. It had recently seen concerts by

Hubbard's Cubbard, Peter Piper and the Magic Harp Rock
Ensemble. Tonight, as we were advised by every billboard
on the way, it was hosting 'An Evening of Classical and Jazz
Fusion by the Experimental Quartet Olé "King" Kohl and
his Fiddlers Three'. That sounded nasty. In musical terms
the word fusion always suggested a number of musicians
all playing completely different tunes at the same time with
their eyes shut, nodding their heads knowingly all the while.
The audience, baffled by what was going on on stage, would
shout phrases like 'nice', 'cool', 'look at those hip cats go'
and even an occasional 'groovy' (the Grimmtown musical
cognoscenti were just as pretentious and anachronistic as
their counterparts everywhere else).

It just made my ears bleed.

Already crowds were arriving for the Fiddlers' Christmas
Eve recital. Had they really nothing better to do with their
time on this particular night? Either that or Kohl and the
boys were more popular than I thought – or expected. As
we pulled into the car park, Mrs C asked a very obvious
question – and one that I'd completely failed to consider.
'How are we going to get in? Do you have tickets for this
gig?'

'It won't be a problem,' I replied, though it was distinctly
possible it might be a very big problem. If the crowds were
anything to go by, this was a sell-out so getting in might be a
tad on the difficult side.

We pushed our way through the crowds, trying to get closer to the door. Two huge figures were checking all the tickets. There would be no way past them – or would there? If I wasn't mistaken, the ticket collectors were my two friends, Lewis and Carroll. They'd certainly deter anyone from trying to get in with a forged ticket or without any ticket at all – unless of course that person was me.

'Stick close,' I whispered. 'We might have a way in after all.' I pushed my way through the throng towards the ticket check, with Mrs C and Basili close behind. They were much better pushers than I was so I skilfully fell behind them and let them do the dirty work. It was like the parting of a human Red Sea; people just disappeared in front of them as they man- (or woman-) handled their way through, clearing out bodies like a flamethrower through a field of snowmen. Getting to the front of the line was easy after that.

Mr Lewis took one look at me and rolled his eyes upwards and gave me an 'I didn't peg you as a jazz buff' look (Mr Lewis was a man of few words).

'I'm not,' I replied. 'But I'm on a case and need to see Kohl as soon as possible.'

Mr Lewis raised an eyebrow in an 'I suppose tickets are out of the question in this instance' expression.

'You know me too well and I really need to get inside.'

Seconds later we were running through the Cauldron's huge lobby, searching for a way backstage. If Kohl was anywhere, he'd be back there getting ready. Everywhere I looked all I could see were doors leading to the auditorium proper; upper stalls, lower stalls, balcony, dress circle. There was no way I'd ever wear a dress just to get a good seat.

I spotted a nervous-looking usher and made a beeline for him. 'How do I get backstage?'

'Um, Mr Kohl doesn't like to be disturbed before he goes on stage. He's very particular about that,' stammered the usher, clearly intimidated by my friends.

'Well, I need to disturb him now and if I don't find a way backstage quickly my associates may very well set about disturbing you.'

The usher pointed to a passageway, partially hidden by a velvet curtain. 'D . . . d . . . down that way.'

'You are most helpful,' I said as we brushed him aside and headed down the passageway. 'Please don't let me find out you warned him we were coming.'

'N . . . n . . . never crossed m . . . my mind,' the usher replied.

'In that case don't ask your face to be a corroborating witness,' I said. 'It mightn't hold up under questioning.'

The passageway led to a dimly lit corridor running the length of the backstage area. On one side were a series of doors, each with a large star in the centre. The first few were blank, but the fourth had 'Mr Kohl and Band' scrawled across it.

'We're here,' I whispered to the others.

'Great,' Mrs C whispered back. 'Now what do we do?'

'Well, let me listen for a moment, see if I can make out who's inside.' Carefully I put my ear to the door and tried to hear what was going on inside. It wasn't difficult; Kohl had a very loud voice.

'We wait until everyone's settled, play a few of the standards and when they're getting into it Santa can do his stuff. Once everything stops we make our way through the audience, relieve them of their valuables and get back on the stage. It's the perfect crime and we'll have the perfect alibi. It's foolproof, I tell you.'

'And what about Santa?' asked another voice. 'He wasn't too easy to persuade last time. What makes you think he'll cooperate again?'

'As long as he thinks we'll let him free in time for Christmas, he'll reluctantly play ball. By the time he finds out I intend to hold on to him, it will be far too late. After that we'll have to find more effective means to ensure his help.'

It was the perfect crime. Looked like we were just in time. If what they were saying was to be believed, Santa was just beyond the door.

I turned to the others and repeated what I'd just heard. 'Just give me a few minutes to come up with a plan.'

Mrs C pushed me aside. 'Plan be damned, I'm going in there,' and before I could stop her she'd flung the door open and barged into the room shouting, 'Santa, where are you? It's me, Clarissa.' Whatever that woman had in terms of devotion to her husband was more than compensated for by her lack of subtlety – and this lack of subtlety had put paid to any chance of a surprise. No sooner had she burst into the room than two of Kohl's Fiddlers Three had grabbed her and flung her back at us. As we fell in a heap like a bunch of oversized skittles, the third grabbed a large red shape that had been lying in the corner, threw it over his shoulder and made for the door with the rest of the band in close pursuit.

'Stop them, they're getting away,' shouted Mrs C at me.

'I'd love to,' I groaned, 'but I should point out that it's difficult just at the moment as you're lying on top of me.'

'Oops, sorry.' She rolled to one side and I sprang (well, struggled) to my feet, dusted myself down and raced down the corridor after them. Considering they had to carry a large body, they were certainly making good progress as there was no sign of them ahead of me.

I burst through a fire door at the end of the corridor and heard them disappear up the stairs in front of me. Stairs; good, that would slow them down a bit. Above me I could hear scuffling as their cargo finally began to weigh heavily on them. I knew I'd never be able to take them on all on my own, but if Jack had managed to deliver his message, well then things might just work out after all.

I'd like to say I raced up the stairs after Kohl, but I'd be lying, or exaggerating at the very least. I was still winded after Mrs C had landed on me and I was also being extra careful to avoid being jumped on by any – or all – of the Fiddlers

Three. This meant that by the time I got to the top of the stairs and out on to the roof of the Cauldron, I was just in time to hear the screaming noise I'd become oh so familiar with recently as Kohl and the boys took off in their private jet sleigh, waving rudely out of the window at me and leaving me standing on the roof watching as they disappeared into the darkening sky.

Or so they thought.

They had barely disappeared from view when I heard a voice from above. 'Harry, are you OK?'

A magic carpet flew down and hovered beside me, Jack peering down over the edge.

'I'm fine, Jack,' I replied. 'Now shift over and give me some room.' I climbed on to the carpet and nodded at Ali Baba. 'You got my message then?'

'Your man was most persuasive.' He waved at the sky. 'Are those the people who framed me for the robbery?'

'They most certainly are, but I haven't really time to explain right now.' I fastened the Velcro strip I'd been handed onto my behind and made sure I was stuck to the carpet. I pointed in the direction the jet sleigh had taken. 'I've always wanted to say this: follow that sleigh.'

Instantly the magic carpet lurched forward and we were about to ascend when there was a shout from below. 'Wait for us.' Basili and Mrs C had finally made their way to the roof, just in time to slow us down.

'Do we wait for them?' asked Ali Baba, looking down at them doubtfully.

'We don't have a choice, I think,' I said. 'It's her husband who's behind all this, so the least we can do is take her with us.'

'Very well,' sighed Ali Baba and indicated for the carpet to stop. Seconds later both Basili and Mrs C had scrambled aboard and the carpet dropped significantly in the air. 'Not good,' I heard Ali Baba mutter under his breath but at least he didn't threaten to push them off again.

Much more slowly this time, the magic carpet ascended into the evening sky and sped after the sleigh. I could just make it out ahead of us, flying back towards the city.

'Quick, we need to catch them before they land,' I shouted pointing at the sleigh.

'That may be easier said than done,' said Ali Baba as his driver tried to urge as much speed as he could out of his cloth vehicle.

Slowly we began to pick up speed but I wasn't sure it would be enough. The sleigh didn't seem to be getting any closer.

'We're not going to catch them, are we?' said a plaintive voice from beside me. 'And it's all my fault.' Mrs C burst into tears once more.

I tried to comfort her (I seemed to spend my time comforting her). 'Don't worry, Ali Baba is a very resourceful man. I'm sure he's working on something even as I speak.'

As if he could hear me from the back of the carpet, Ali Baba said, 'We're not going to catch them. I am sorry, Harry; we are just carrying too much weight.' This provoked a new flood of tears from Mrs C, and it certainly wasn't what I'd hoped he was going to say.

'Perhaps I might be of some assistance,' said a voice from somewhere on my left. As I was sitting on the leftmost edge of the magic carpet it was fair to say that this was something I hadn't expected. As I looked around we were bathed in a bright red light and I looked straight into the eyes of Rudolph the Red-nosed Reindeer.

'What in the name of blazes are you doing here?' I asked.

'Clarissa thought I might be of help, so I got here as quickly as I could,' he replied.

'What, you think you might be able to pull us along, do you?' I wasn't sure exactly how this arrogant animal could be of any use whatsoever bearing in mind our last meeting so I didn't want to waste my time on him.

'Don't be ludicrous, my dear pig. I see no point in pulling this particular craft.' Rudolph was confirming my suspicions all the while but then, just when I figured all he was going to do was to give us vocal encouragement, he surprised me. 'But I might be able to carry a passenger on my back.'

'If you do, do you think you can catch them?' I asked.

'What do you think I do for a living every Christmas Eve? Of course I can catch them. Now are you going to hop on or not?'

Was he talking to me? He was certainly looking at me. Why was it always me that got asked these questions? Was I really seen as some kind of superhero? Everyone on the magic carpet was looking at me too – most of them with 'I'm glad I wasn't asked' expressions on their faces.

With a resigned groan I peeled off the Velcro and stood up. 'OK, Rudolph, I guess it's up to you and me now. Get close to the carpet so I can climb on your back without falling off.'

Rudolph taxied in and flew parallel to the carpet. Ever so carefully I stepped off the ornate material and on to Rudolph's back. As I did so, he turned his head and whispered, 'This never happened, is that clear? Under no circumstances should anyone ever find out I did this. It's so humiliating.'

Clinging tightly to his neck, I whispered back, 'Heigh-ho, Rudolph, away.'

16

Get Behind Me Santa

I'll give Rudolph credit for one thing: he was fast. In a matter of seconds he'd left the magic carpet far behind and was speeding over Grimmtown in hot pursuit of Kohl. I suppose speed was of the essence if you had to get around the world delivering presents over the course of one night, time being stopped or not. The drawback with this incredible burst of speed was that he had me on his back and I had nothing to hold on to by way of saddle or reins. It meant I had to get closer to Rudolph than I would have wished; wrapping my arms tightly around his neck and pressing my legs firmly against his body. With the wind threatening to drag me off and throw me away, trust me, I was clinging on with whatever bits of my body I could use. At least Rudolph smelled nice. I'd expected something mangy and pungent, but, considering how he'd been when I'd first met him, I shouldn't have been surprised that he exuded a scent of aromatic oils and expensive cosmetics.

Rudolph must have felt my panic – then again my legs were probably on the point of crushing his ribs so it wasn't too hard to miss. 'I don't suppose you could relax a little? You're not making this very easy for me,' he asked.

'Believe me, from where I'm sitting it's not too much fun for me either, but don't take it personally; it's not like we're engaged or anything.'

All I got in return was an indignant snort, but I did try to relax my vice-like grip a little – but only a little. From where I sat, it was a long trip to the ground and there were no return tickets if I slipped off.

Rudolph wove in and out through Grimmtown's sky-scrapers like a supersonic bee in a flower garden, always keeping the sleigh in his sights. As far as I could make out we were beginning to gain on it – not that I spent too much time looking; mostly my head was buried in Rudolph's neck.

I leaned forward towards Rudolph's head once more. 'Are we there yet?'

'We're catching up. Whatever you've planned, be ready to do it shortly.'

Now that we were getting closer I realised that I hadn't really thought through what I was going to do next. Even if we did catch up with the sleigh, we were still hundreds of feet above the ground and lacking in certain key accessories: namely a parachute, a weapon of some sort, a way into the sleigh and, most importantly, a soft landing should things go wrong. Looked like once more I'd be making it up as I went along, only this time I couldn't afford to make any mistakes – at least not if I didn't want to spend yet more time doing some unforced mid-air acrobatics.

I took a quick glance ahead; we were slightly behind and just above Kohl's sleigh. Rudolph had done fantastically well to catch up.

From above there didn't seem like there was any way into it – not that I suspected there'd be an easy way in regardless of what angle we approached it.

'Take us down beside it,' I ordered. 'I need to take a closer look.'

Rudolph obliged and flew parallel to the craft. There was a door in the side, but I wasn't sure I'd be able – or even wanted – to try to do a mid-air reindeer to sleigh transfer and open that door from the outside. Scratch that. There was only one option left.

'Let's have a look at what's underneath.'

Seconds later we were looking up at the undercarriage. This one was different from the others I'd seen in that it looked to have landing gear as opposed to skis.

'That's because it's geared for urban flying rather than polar,' Rudolph advised. 'They're becoming very popular with Grimmtown's rich set.'

'No doubt,' I replied, scanning the underside of the craft carefully. Like all the other sides there didn't seem to be any obvious entry point. The wheels nestled snugly against the surface and didn't offer any way in – not that I was prepared to try that particular route; I wasn't a slim pig and I don't think I'd have managed to squeeze through. I didn't even want to contemplate what would happen if the wheels suddenly came down while I was clambering over them. The beginnings of a plan were forming in my head, but I had to find a way in in order to make it work. If they managed to get back on to the ground I'd be sunk.

I was just about to order Rudolph away from the sleigh and have a rethink when I saw a small handle nestling snugly against the sleigh's underbelly. Urging Rudolph closer, I had a better look. It seemed to provide access to some sort of undercarriage maintenance area. If there was a way in, there just might be a way up into the sleigh proper.

'I'm going to try to open that hatch,' I told Rudolph. 'Keep an eye on me when it swings out. The last thing I need right now is some freefall training.'

Rudolph nodded and rose up against the hatch. I grabbed the handle, twisted it and pulled. The door swung down, revealing . . . well, um, a dark space actually. Without a torch I had no way of seeing what was in there. Oh well, why would this be any different from any other time?

Now came the tricky bit. As carefully as I could, I pushed myself on to my knees and then stood on Rudolph's back. 'Whatever you do, don't wobble or suddenly decide to fly away, OK?' I told him. I slowly reached up, grabbed the edge of the hatch and, with Rudolph's help, climbed into the darkness. 'Do me a favour and stick your head in here,' I shouted down to him. Seconds later, he poked his head in and the area was illuminated by a red light. Who needs a torch when you've a red-nosed reindeer?

The maintenance area itself was small and just allowed a mechanic access to the landing gear. There wasn't even room to stand up but once I was inside and crouching I saw another hatch in the roof above me. Figuring that this might open out into the sleigh proper, I cracked it open and peered through the narrow slit. I could hear laughing from the cabin above. Clearly Kohl and the boys figured they were home and hosed. All I could see through the crack were the band members' feet – and they did have very nice shoes indeed – but I imagined the rest of the band were attached to them too, so jumping into the cabin and attempting a rescue was probably out of the question unless . . .

I poked my head back down and called to Rudolph. 'Count to twenty and then cause a diversion.'

'Whatever do you mean? What kind of diversion? I'm Santa's lead reindeer you know, not some sort of performing animal,' a highly indignant Rudolph replied.

'Well, if you want to hold on to that job then you need to do something to distract the people in this sleigh so I can rescue Santa. Do I make myself clear?'

Rudolph nodded. 'Absolutely.'

'Good, start counting now.' Rudolph disappeared from view and began to count. I hoped he'd come up with something that would attract the attention of everyone in the sleigh otherwise it would the worst rescue in the history of bad rescues.

Seventeen . . . eighteen . . . nineteen . . . twenty. I cracked open the hatch once more and waited. It wasn't a long wait. I'd barely finished the count when I heard excited shouts from above.

'Hey, what's that flying in front of us?' said a voice.

'Dunno, it looks like a big dog,' said another. I sincerely hoped Rudolph couldn't hear; I wasn't sure quite how his ego would take that remark.

'Now what's he doing?' Whatever it was I hoped it was going to be good.

'Hey, guys, come take at look at this.'

This was followed by the sound of fading footsteps as what I hoped was every member of King Kohl and his Fiddlers Three charged up front for a look.

I pushed up the hatch, clambered into the cabin and looked around. I was instantly drawn to the red shape slumped in the corner.

Santa – and he was unguarded. I ran over to him and shook him. 'Santa, wake up.' There was no reaction. I slapped him gently on the face – still nothing.

There was a shocked voice from the cockpit. 'Oh no, he cannot be serious.'

This was followed by, 'There's no way he's going to do that.'

'Oh my God, he is.'

'That's disgusting,' and finally, 'It's going to hit, taking evasive action.'

Then the plane lurched sideways. Wow, whatever Rudolph was doing, it was certainly working. All I had to do now was wake Santa up and I could put the last piece of my plan into action. The plane bucked wildly again and I was flung across the cabin. Seconds later a still unconscious Santa fell on top of me.

Panic reigned in the cockpit. 'I can't see a thing; the whole window is covered in poo. It's like tar. What did that dog have for lunch and how the hell are we going to get it off?'

I pushed Santa off me and shook him once more. He mumbled something incomprehensible and slowly opened his eyes.

'Aren't you a little short to be a member of Fiddlers Three?' he slurred.

'I'm Harry Pigg and I've come to rescue you.'

'You're who?'

'I'm Harry Pigg,' I repeated. 'Your wife sent me. I'm here with Rudolph.'

Comprehension began to register in Santa's befuddled brain. 'Rudolph, where is he?'

'He's outside, come on.' I pulled Santa to his feet and draped his arm over my shoulder. Slowly I dragged him

157

across to the hatch and, yes I'm ashamed to admit it, I just dropped him in. Seconds later, I fell in beside him and pulled the hatch shut.

'Now what?' asked Santa.

'Now we wait for your pal to come back, which should be any second now.'

No sooner had I spoken that we were immersed in a red glow once more. 'Under no circumstances is anyone ever to know what I did to divert those people, understood?' said a somewhat shamefaced Rudolph.

'My lips are sealed,' I said with a smirk. 'Now,' I turned to Santa, 'how does this stopping time trick of yours work?'

'You know about that?' said Santa indignantly. 'How did you find out?'

'I'm a detective, it's what I do,' I said, and then as an afterthought, 'trust me, your people didn't tell me; I worked it out for myself.'

Santa gave me a disbelieving look but, after a few seconds' consideration, let it slide – at least for the moment. 'Here's how it works: you have to be touching me so you won't be affected when everything stops then all I do is—'

There was a pounding noise from above. Santa's disappearance had been discovered. We didn't have much time. I grabbed Santa by the hand and held on to Rudolph's nose with my other trotter. The reindeer gave an indignant squeal. 'Now would be a good time, Santa,' I said, raising my eyes to the commotion above. Santa nodded once to show he understood and closed his eyes.

The hatch was ripped open and tuxedo bedecked arms stretched in, trying to grab us.

'Right now would be even better,' I squealed as hands scrabbled at my head.

Almost immediately the noise from above stopped. Santa opened his eyes once more. 'That's it,' he smiled.

'That's it?' I said. 'You just close your eyes and, hey presto, time stops?'

'I've had hundreds of years of practice,' Santa replied. 'Mind you it's not quite as easy as it looks. Now I really think we should be going.'

'No argument from me.' I hopped on to Rudolph's back and helped Santa on in front of me. 'I couldn't agree more.'

Seconds later we dropped out of the hatch and flew back in the direction of the City once more.

It was an eerie sensation, flying through the night when everything around us had stopped dead still. Kohl's sleigh hung suspended in the sky like a giant Christmas tree ornament and all around us everything was silent. Below, the lights of Grimmtown's evening traffic were unmoving. The landscape looked like a giant version of Santa's house.

Once we were far enough away from the sleigh I said to Santa, 'I think we're OK now.' There was a rush of air and suddenly we were surrounded by the noise of the traffic below, the wind whistling around our faces and the distant screaming of Kohl's jet sleigh as it staggered through the sky while the passengers tried to figure out some way of clearing the poo from the cockpit windows before it crashed – and no doubt trying to figure out exactly where we'd disappeared to.

'Not long now,' I shouted at Santa, trying to make myself heard over the buffeting wind.

Santa turned back to reply and was about to say something when his face dropped. 'I'm not so sure about that,' he said pointing back over my shoulder, concern visible on his face. I swung around and saw Kohl's jet sleigh bearing down on us. Through a smeared windscreen I could see the pilot grinning as the aircraft rapidly closed the distance between us.

'Rudolph,' I roared, 'you need to get a move on. They're right behind us.'

'I'll do my best,' Rudolph puffed. 'But my load is somewhat heavier now; I'm not sure how long I'll be able to keep it up.'

'Just do your best, I'll think of something.' Though I wasn't quite sure what. This time there didn't seem to be an obvious way out. Kohl's sleigh was just too big and too fast. I remembered the damage the other one had done to our sleigh on the way to the North Pole, so I didn't think one Santa, one reindeer and an – admittedly brilliant – pig detective would offer much by way of resistance if they chose to ram us, which I reckoned would be any second now.

It was obvious that Rudolph was tiring. His flight pattern was becoming more erratic and he was beginning to wheeze.

All the while our pursuers were chewing up the distance between us. I looked behind me once more. They were right on top of us. This was it – we were going to die. They were so close I could see Kohl in the cockpit mouthing 'I have you now' at me.

There was a sudden blur of movement and something flew in between us and the sleigh. Caught by surprise, the pilot spun away wildly, careening out of control into the sky above.

What had happened? I looked around and then heard Jack Horner's voice from underneath us, 'Woohoo, you're all clear, Harry. Now let's drop Santa off and wrap this thing up.'

I looked down and saw Ali Baba's carpet flying along below us. A smiling Jack gave me a thumbs up and a very relieved-looking Mrs C applauded wildly.

'Thank you,' she mouthed and I gave a small bow in acknowledgement and almost fell off Rudolph as a consequence.

Note to self: never try flashy gestures when balancing on the back of a tiring reindeer several hundred feet above the ground.

17

Happy Christmas to All, and to All a Good Wrap Up

Two days later I was back at work.

What about holidays? I hear you say, but a detective's work is never done. Anyway, I was looking for something to occupy myself. Having spent Christmas in close proximity to a flatulent ex-genie who snored like a foghorn had left me understandably eager to get out of the apartment.

Once more I was in the office, feet up on my desk, enjoying the silence (and the lack of unpleasant odours). At the other side of the desk, Jack Horner was showing me what he'd got from Santa, which, considering the part he'd played in the rescue, was a substantial haul indeed. Apparently his mother had been more than a little surprised at the amount of gear heaped under the Horner tree on Christmas morning.

I was basking in the satisfaction of a job well done. Santa had been delivered back to the North Pole just before midnight, just in time to commence deliveries. I'd asked him how long the job would take once he'd frozen time and set off on his journey.

'About twenty-four years, give or take a day or so. Our record is twenty-one years, three months, two days and twelve seconds but we were much younger then,' he'd said, a tad ruefully.

'Let me get this straight. Every Christmas Eve it takes you about twenty-five years to get around the world, delivering presents to everyone then you get home and start the whole thing all over again?'

'That's about right, yes.'

Wow, and I thought I had a tough job.

Jack's chattering interrupted my thoughts.

'Harry, there's a few things I don't understand.'

'Yes,' I said.

'Well, Kohl got away, didn't he? Won't the police lock up Ali Baba 'cause they still think he did it?'

'They still suspect him, that's true, but now that he knows Kohl did it, he can ensure enough evidence is planted at the various crime scenes to incriminate him.'

'You mean he's going to frame him?' Jack sounded indignant.

'Well, I don't think it's considered framing someone when they've actually committed the crime, do you?'

'I suppose not,' said Jack doubtfully. 'But what about Danny Emperor?'

'Well, you can imagine his surprise when he went to his warehouse yesterday and everything had been put back exactly where it had been before Ali Baba had taken it. That was the deal I made with Ali and, in fairness to him, he stuck to it. Danny still has a faint suspicion he might have hallucinated the robbery and who am I to dissuade him from that thought? At least we got a few suits for Basili out of it, seeing as Danny was so grateful.'

'Yeah, that's not a bad thing. Basili's yellow outfit is a bit . . . um . . . loud.'

I stood up and slapped Jack on the shoulder. 'That's true,' I laughed. 'Come on, let me buy you lunch.'

Jack sat there with a frown on his face. 'There's one thing that I don't understand though.'

'Only one?'

Jack ignored my insult. 'Well, if the time travel thing is such a big secret and only the Santas know about it, apart from us, of course,' he said.

'Yes?'

'How then did Kohl know about it? He had to know about it in order to carry out the robberies in the first place, didn't he?'

'You know, Jack, that's a very good question.' It was a very good question – and one I'd spent quite an amount of time thinking about over the previous few days. I wasn't going to tell Jack, but I had a sneaking suspicion that there was more going on here than we knew about. Somebody had tipped Kohl off and I didn't think that somebody was Santa or anyone in his immediate circle. Something told me we hadn't even begun to scratch the surface of this particular mystery. Call it a hunch if you like but my detective senses had been tingling since Christmas Eve. Something was brewing; I was certain of it and this case had only been the beginning. There was more to what went on than met the eye and I was convinced that I was going to be involved whether I liked it or not.

But today wasn't the day to be worrying about it. I needed to treat Jack to a well-earned lunch.

We were on our way out of my office when there was a timid knock on the door.

There goes lunch, I thought.

I opened the door to a very petite, very pale and very obviously frightened young woman.

'Can I help you, madam?' I asked.

The woman was clearly on the verge of tears.

Not another one, I thought. Why do they gravitate towards me?

'Please, Mr Pigg, I need your help. My name is Muffet, Matilda Muffet, and I'm having a terrible spider problem.'

The End
The Third Pig Detective Agency will return
in
The Curds and Whey Mystery

Acknowledgements

Again, a whole raft of people contributed hugely to getting this book on the shelves.

As always, thanks are due to Scott and Corinna at The Friday Project for their work in making *The Ho Ho Ho Mystery* presentable in the first place. The comments that came with with the edits were worth the admission price alone!

To my agent, Svetlana, for the support, advice and help and for educating me in the mysterious and arcane ways of the publishing industry – and she makes great jam too.

To all those who offered help, advice and assistance over the past few years: Darren Craske (great writer, buy his books now), Guy Saville (great writer, buy his book when it comes out in 2011), all at CBI, David Maybury, Dooradoyle and Adare libraries (again), and all those places around Limerick that have great coffee and a quite corner to write in. It all adds up folks.

Above all, thanks to my family, Gemma, Ian, Adam and Stephen for 'encouraging me' to be in front of the computer at 9:30 every day and for ensuring my feet were firmly fixed on the ground during the process. No chance of any airs and graces with you lot around!

Ian: please be advised that beating me once at Pro Evo Soccer does not make you better than me.

Adam: Bazinga!

Stephen: they won the Premiership and the FA Cup, Drogba ended up the top scorer by a country mile, isn't it about time you admitted that Chelsea are far superior to Manchester United in every way? No? All right then, they'll just have to do it again.